# ROMEO &
# SEAHORSE

Published in 2024 by Cipher Press

203 Ryan House
12 Smeed Road
London, E3 2PE

First published in Denmark in 2022 by Gladiator

Paperback ISBN: 978-1-917008-04-4
eBook ISBN: 978-1-917008-05-1

Printed and bound in the UK by TJ Books

Distributed by Turnaround Publisher Services

Edited by Jakob Sandvad & Jack Thompson
Cover Design by Wolf
Typeset by Laura Jones-Rivera

This book is a work of fiction,
and we trust you all to know what this means

www.cipherpress.co.uk

# ROMEO & SEAHORSE

## NIKOLAJ TANGE LANGE

Cipher
press

I just told my boyfriend I have Hepatitis C again. He was sitting on the sofa when they called from my doctor and he could tell right away that something was wrong, so there was no way around just telling it as it is. He didn't understand how I could've got it again already. Not after I promised I'd take better care of myself. I said that maybe I'd used someone else's straw by accident when sniffing speed, since it seemed like the most innocent explanation. Fortunately he didn't ask how many times I've had it by now, because, to be honest, I don't remember what I told him before. I also don't remember how many times I've actually had it, but in the fourteen years since I moved to Berlin, it's probably been around a handful. I still think I should've been able to suppress my reaction when they called this morning. I can't say it came as a surprise, not with the way I've fucked up with Tina lately. Most people know her as crystal meth or methamphetamine, but among friends, it's always just Tina. It's a way of lying to ourselves to make the addiction sound less serious. I lie to my boyfriend, I lie to my friends, I lie to my doctor who I'm otherwise always honest with. Did I do drugs? Yes. Did we use condoms? No. Did I take part in group sex or sex parties? Yes. Did I get fisted? Yes. Did we use gloves? Not every time. Did I get fucked by dildos or other things that were inside others before me? Probably, yes. Should we test for Chlamydia and Gonorrhoea? Yes please. For Syphilis? Yes please. Hepatitis C? Yes please. But on Wednesday, when he asked if I'd had any contact with Tina, I couldn't bring myself to admit it. The same goes for my boyfriend; he knows about most guys I'm with, a lot of them at least, but I've never been able to tell him about Tina. I send him messages while my phone is melting in my hand, live updates from my own destruction, to tell him we're just hanging out. Just chilling. I lie about why I'm gone for so long, why I sleep so bad, why there's so little left of me. In the end I guess I'm mostly lying to myself, but I'm getting sidetracked here since it's not drugs or disease I want to write about but the love I still believe can conquer everything.

I've seen in pictures that my mum and dad used to be happy together. Slides that were usually stowed away in grey plastic boxes, that were only brought out on special occasions and shown to my sister and me. Staring into the living room wall as my father controlled the chopping of the projector, box after box, tray after tray, through endless summer days in a flowery hippie van, me in cotton diapers and a purple corduroy sling, my sister still only there in ideas of what we were to become. When I otherwise think of my mum and dad together, I mostly remember how they fought. How they yelled, pushed, or attacked each other. My dad who'd been caught lying about his overtime, my mum who'd found out about another one of his affairs. I remember once my sister and I had both gotten a pencil holder made out of plastic, hers in red and mine in blue, and while they were fighting my sister's got thrown so hard against the wall that it shattered. I don't remember who threw it, if it was thrown in attack or defence, I just remember how my sister stood there, crying with red plastic splinters between her fingers, and how they kept on fighting as my mother tried to comfort her, and though it wasn't like this all the time it's mostly how I remember it, since some memories carve deeper than others.

In the end, I probably just think that if we're not gonna fuck and drink poison together, I'm not sure I see the point.

Vincent texts and asks me what I'm doing tonight. At first I don't know how to answer, or yes, actually I do, since I was so prepared for the Hepatitis test to be positive that I long ago decided he must have it too. I go to him, and he opens the door to his flat half naked as usual, just one big room with a double bed, a desk, and a concrete grey sofa which he always tries to keep covered with towels though the fabric underneath is as foul as a darkroom floor on Sunday morning. I offer him a hug as usual, and a dry kiss on the mouth as usual, and I still can't believe how skinny he is, how his butt can be so tiny it barely holds up his jockstrap. The glass pipe lies ready on his desk as usual, I embrace it from across the room as usual, then do my best to ignore it till I'm invited since I want to hold on to the idea that it isn't Tina I'm here for. I try to listen when he asks me how I'm doing but it's hard when, at the same time, I have Tina in my ear, her whisper telling me I'm horny, and Tina always has her way, no questions, just demands about everything all at once. But now that I've made it this far, through the never-ending February night (from Neukölln in the east of Berlin to Wilmersdorf way out west), through this steel-jawed night, this zero-fucks night, I'll probably get through this last bit too, even though I'm already dead on my feet from sitting there on the bus, staring into my own frosty breath, counting the minutes and the stops while the pipe just lay here pulling my body towards it like a black hole, and I sincerely wished the way here wasn't always this constant humiliation, that my fall wouldn't have to be on display on a bus through the entire city, that I could just let go and give in to this force that, in the end, is always gonna win. He asks about my day, and I say it's been chill, I ask about his, and he says the same, and I wonder what he does when he's not having sex and taking drugs because the flat feels like a hamster cage set up for sex and drugs, for crawling to the bed for a quick blackout (just until you're fit enough to crawl back and get on with the grind), and I don't find it unlikely that his life is just one big hamster wheel of sex and drugs and blackouts, while I at least still have some sort of everyday life where I get up and walk around on two legs or sit down with my laptop to make myself believe that I'm working, though I mostly end up just browsing the hook-up sites and all sorts of other crap on the internet, and I still have my boyfriend to try and be something for, and even though I often curse the lies I have to pull out every time I come home, he's also my lifeline, since it's exactly the lies I hold on to when I'm with him that keep me from slipping away into darkness forever. I'm being asked if I have any wishes for porn as he scrolls down an endless array of previews, of tattooed muscle bodies (his own in front of the screen more like an anorexic teenager's though he's turning thirty soon), and I tell him he can just pick whatever he wants, and he clicks on an image of three guys going at it on a white IKEA sofa, which I'm sure will be tossed out after they're done, and I pull out Seahorse, my favourite dildo, which is bigger than both his hands together, a severed dragon dick I lay out on one of his towels along with poppers and lube (a rose is a rose, a hole is a hole, and a dildo is sometimes just a dildo, but my Seahorse is still something quite special to me), and I undress while he pulls out a stack of flattened moving boxes from under the bed and starts covering the floor so we'll have something to slide around on once we get started, slide in and out of each other and in and out of consciousness the way we usually do once we get started; it's still just preparations we're treading through, because until I've sucked on that pipe, there's really nothing pulling us toward each other, not until he tells me, so terribly soon I can barely be in my own body, (as if it's really nothing special) that I'm welcome to smoke a bit if I want, because that's what Tina can do for us, she can crush us in her arms and turn us into boiling liquids, prepare us to be mixed and poured into whichever mould that fits. It's only been two months since we first met and I didn't know what kind of drugs he did, back then I just said yes to one puff without knowing what weight his charred little crystal dick could carry, but already with the second puff the sparks started jumping, I was a stick of Acme dynamite, I was Bugs Bunny running over the edge of the cliff and as long as I didn't look down I could keep on running, and this is how it's always been with Tina, this is why I don't say no now, this is why I don't want to say no now, this is why I never was able to say no, but where I used to go for months without giving in to her, we've been sucking the life out of each other every single weekend since New Year's, and I know the first puff is no longer a stick of dynamite but rather just relief from the clamp that's been pressing hard on my skull this whole week, relief that I can finally feel normal again, and actually I shouldn't even be here now, or yes, I should, but I should stop this thing and tell him about my Hepatitis test, though in the end I can't imagine he also doesn't have it, especially after that weekend three weeks ago when he invited that other guy over as well, the one who messaged me afterwards and said he had Gonorrhoea, Chlamydia, and Syphilis, which was why I'd gone to the doctor as well, because all three of us had been punching away inside each other and none of us stopped because of a little blood so if one of us has Hepatitis now it's hard to imagine we don't all have Hepatitis now, and in this case, bringing out the gloves is just a little too late. I wish we could talk about it openly but I already tried this, and back then I was put on ice for nine months until I was safe again, because why rely on latex when you can just search for another hole to play with, and when the game is all about digging tunnels through each other and putting our brains on hold as we do it, there's really no room for thoughts about safety; the virus we learnt to fear is harmless now (an Eighties thing, a retro virus, a vintage T-shirt that says silence = death, bought in a hipster shop that used to house a community kitchen), and we made a pact now to never talk of disease again, only to tell each other we better get checked for Gonorrhoea, Chlamydia, or Syphilis, and as long as we take the pills we're prescribed none of them really affect us, with the exception of Hepatitis C, which is why that name can never be mentioned, because it undermines every risk assessment and threatens our ability to turn a blind eye and still look ourselves in the mirror. I tell myself it's quite likely he's had it since we started seeing each other, that he also couldn't say it out loud, or maybe it was the other guy he invited over, the one who also had Gonorrhoea, Chlamydia, and Syphilis, and he could easily have known the entire time but not been able to say it out loud, or say that we better use gloves, and in this way it's really their fault that I have it now, and all the others who silently agreed that Hepatitis C is not something we can talk about, it's their silence that made me sick, and this is why they deserve to get it too, and this is why I'm staying silent now, just waiting for a green light to run over the edge, fall down on his sofa and let him punch me from the inside till he's all beat, till his fists come tumbling back out, tired and covered in pink mucus, curled up and fragile like freshly hatched birdlings.

One of the few good memories I have of my mum and my dad together is when we all had to go out in the evening, and we'd get ready in their bedroom upstairs. My mum would pick out jewellery and do her make-up in front of her dressing table, which was beautifully carved with floral patterns and an oval mirror in the middle where she tried on her jewellery while my dad moved around doing whatever men do when they have to look fancy, which was harder to put a finger on except that he always needed help with his tie, and my sister and I sat together on their bed in our fanciest threads, and even though we were all the same as usual, everything seemed somehow more refined, like when plain ordinary groceries are arranged in a basket with cellophane and a bow around them. One day when we had to go out in the evening, I heard voices from the bedroom upstairs and got scared they'd already started without me. I raced as fast as I could up the stairs, but halfway up my socks slipped under me, I fell and knocked my brand new front tooth down on the hardwood steps, and my mum and my dad came rushing down and picked me up, tried to comfort me and made sure I wasn't hurt apart from the chip they immediately saw on my front tooth, a chip that stayed visible for many years and hurt every time I ran my tongue over it, but when I remember myself wailing on the stairs back then, it wasn't at all about my tooth but about how stupid and clumsy I felt for having ruined one of the few good moments we had together.

I started this book with a lie I'd like to take back now. My doctor just called and said my latest Hepatitis test was negative, and he never called and said anything else, not this time at least. I never meant to lie about it, but Wednesday, after I came home from the test, I was so convinced it'd be positive I saw no reason to wait for the result before writing about it. It was actually a relief to write as if I'd already tested positive, and I had no problem writing about meeting Vincent either, since there was never any doubt I'd be meeting Vincent without telling him I tested positive, and now that I admitted this it would feel like a bigger lie to delete it again. But now it's Vincent who cancelled on me tonight and I assume it's about him having stayed up with Tina for days again, so now it's up to me to find another hole I can crash down and fall apart inside.

The Polish skinhead picks me up in front of Penny Markt and we walk together to his flat just across the street. He's one of those people I used to run into at bars and at parties back when I still went out and ran into people, but this is the first time I visit him at home. It's ten o'clock in the evening, and he texted to tell me he just woke up, so I already figured that last night was a heavy one, but when I see him I'm still disturbed by the smell of vodka and the red spots all over his face and all over his shaved head, like little poisoned wounds, and I can't help but wonder if he also got it on with Tina, but assume he mostly just gets it on with whatever he can get his hand on. His Polish friend is there too, and they put on the TV and play a cartoon from YouTube where an onion is dancing to Polish country music and singing a song about crying, and they try to translate the lyrics as the video plays, while pouring vodka shots and mixing them with raspberry syrup. The room feels too hot and too cramped, like we're sitting in an IKEA display room with our coats on, and he keeps talking about his boyfriend or his flat-mate or his boyfriend, I can't keep track of their arrangement, but either way, the boyfriend or flat-mate disappeared this morning, and suddenly his phone showed up 200 kilometres away, and they're pretty sure he found someone who's into smearing shit all over each other while fucking since this is usually what it's about when he suddenly disappears like this. He goes and gets a small plate of drugs, it's just speed and ecstasy, and I'm disappointed, and I'm relieved at the same time because now I can get high on something that isn't Tina and act like it's my decision that it isn't Tina, even though of course I hoped it would be Tina, but now it's not, and it's also fine like this. The speed is all dried up like a lump of chalk on the plate (a memory of the White Cliffs of Denmark). He scrapes it with a frayed health insurance card, forms six fat lines which we snort two of each. He splits a diamond-shaped pill down the middle, swallows one half and hands me the other, and he calls me a pussy when I bite my half, but fifteen minutes later when he's rolling back and forth on the sofa while a twinky DJ in yellow neon clothes jumps up and down in ecstasy over his own music inside the TV, I'm happy I only took a quarter. He pulls down his pants and tugs at his half-erect penis while his Polish friend sleeps in an armchair, and I say that if he wants me to get naked too, he just has to tell me since he already told me I make him horny, but I don't have the patience for how slow this is going, so I grab Seahorse from my backpack as soon as I have my pants off, and I don't even need a minute before I'm all the way down. His eyes are about to roll from their sockets and onto the towels he must've spread out before I arrived, but just as he's sitting there rolling back and forth on his own sofa, his friend or boyfriend or flatmate or whatever he is enters the flat, and an interrogation begins, mostly about how he'd just disappeared without saying a word (that it was about smearing shit all over each other is apparently taken for granted), but actually this had been planned long ago he says, and also it'd been mentioned several times as someone would know if he paid any sort of attention, but he can't be bothered to have this talk right now, and really it's no one's business what he gets up to, and it's clear that even though they try and pretend like they're just teasing each other, it's totally a fight they're having, and suddenly sitting there between them with a ten-centimetre wide dildo up my butt doesn't feel super nice anymore. Fortunately the flatmate or boyfriend or whatever he is just wants to sleep, and as soon as he's out of the room I get up from Seahorse, but the pill and the speed have already done a number on my bowels; a stream of yellow faeces squirts all over the towels, and a stream of excuses flows from my mouth, but he just shushes and quickly wraps up the towels and takes them to the balcony. The only thing he worries about, he explains afterwards, is that the smell won't spread to the bedroom because then his boyfriend or flatmate is just gonna wake up and feel horny, and there's a reason why he has to take these urges elsewhere. The Polish friend wakes up and goes to the bedroom too to continue his sleep, but then a new Polish friend with the same name as the one before shows up, and then we have to watch the cartoon with the onion again, and they try again to explain why it's funny, and he splits another pill in two, and I say I only need a quarter but swallow one of the halves anyway, and we wash it down with pure vodka now, and suddenly it's as if I remember lying at the feet of the Polish friend with Seahorse up my butt, and I can't tell how long it's been, but they both smile like I'm some sort of magical super creature, and I try to say something, but the Polish friend just smiles all over the place till I finally realize he doesn't understand anything but Polish. I pull out Seahorse from my butt, and more yellow faeces squirt out over a new deck of towels, and again he rushes to the balcony with it all so the smell won't reach his boyfriend or flatmate, and he says I need to take better care now since they're out of clean towels, and then we just sit around for a while sniffing speed and drinking vodka, and I cruise for a fisting date on my phone while I entertain them with Danish music videos from YouTube, and they say that all Danes look like faggots and are sure they saw the singer from Søn get fucked in a sling in a sex club, but I say they probably just saw someone who looks like him, or he looks like someone they wish they could fuck themselves. As the morning wears on, a fisting date finally comes through when the Ukrainian skinhead I hooked up with one time last year responds, and I tell the others I'm totally wrecked, though actually I'm trying to get wrecked a whole lot more, but for that I'll need Tina, and I know she's with the Ukrainian skinhead, and that's why I already feel lost inside him on the U-Bahn on my way to his flat and throw off my clothes as soon as I'm inside the door, let the crystals boil in his pipe and fill my lungs till they can take no more, hold it in as I count to ten and let go of a thick white fog, then fill them again and let him dress me in rubber because this is the way he wants me, and he can have me any way he wants as long as I get to fill my lungs again and again, because the satisfaction is already mixed with a let-down that it's no longer the same full steam over the edge as back when I was just trying it out, and that's why I keep filling my lungs and only pretend to think twice when he asks if I slam, and he asks how much, laughs and calls it a baby dose when I say zero point one because he always does zero point two-two, and I end up putting zero point one-two in my own syringe, the highest dose I've ever done (I want to make sure any thoughts I'm having are eaten up by the desire to be torn up from inside), but when he unties the rubber tube from my arm and the crystal liquid rushes into my blood, I'm again disappointed that I have to use my own free will to spread my legs for him, that it doesn't just happen automatically, that I even have a free will and can think about what to do with it, and if next time, maybe I should go up to zero point one-five.

First time I got concerned if my consumption was becoming an addiction was at my doctor's. I go there at least every three months to have my blood checked, checked to make sure my HIV medication is working, checked for Syphilis, checked for Hepatitis C, checked for everything else I'm in a high-risk population for. It's always the same routine; first they ask if I want to lie down or sit, I say sitting works just fine, then they send me to one of their private cubicles and ask me to wait for a moment. They come in with a small plastic tray full of syringes in different sizes, they ask me how I'm doing, if I know how heavy I am, if my right or my left arm is better, and since I don't care about this they just take whichever one is closer, tell me it's gonna get a bit cold now before they spray a couple of times with the disinfectant, tie an elastic band around my upper arm and prepare the needle while they comment on my tattoos or on the weather, but whereas I used to be afraid of the needle and sat there pinching myself with the opposite hand while waiting for the prick, this one time I was suddenly overcome by a feeling of actually longing for the needle, as if every cell in my body were a stupid little dog that starts to drool as soon as it hears the rattling of syringes, and though I know they never have treats for me, I now can't prevent my body from feeling the rush when the needle connects to the vein, and on top of the rush, the let-down when the elastic band is released and nothing happens except that my blood runs quietly down and fills one plastic tube after the other.

I always knew I had to get away as soon as I was out of school because the love I needed could not be found at home, and as another smalltown boy, I packed my things and ran away; the classic tale of becoming a New York City boy or going west to San Francisco where the skies are blue and dreams have space to grow. Some just want to get lost in the crowd, others in the night, become another grey cat in the dark, but for me it was always about love. It was about finding a Romeo I could love so deeply that everyone would know I was a Romeo, too. I imagined my longing for a Romeo to be way more sophisticated than whatever drove other men to make wives of their girlfriends, have children and lock themselves in houses with driveways and gardens around them; our love would be a thorn in the side of the men and the wives in their houses who thought that love could only grow with a fence around it. We would wish a plague upon their houses and raise a love so great it would have a long and prosperous life, long after death had done its part. My contempt for the village I ran from was so great that I sometimes wonder what came first, was it homosexual desire that made me steer away from the ordinary, or was my sexuality already shaped by a more fundamental desire to be different from the others, and though most people probably see the first explanation as the obvious one, I like to believe that it's not necessarily that simple, that it could be like Malene Monka's PhD thesis from 2013 on mobility and dialects, where she shows how adolescents who later move away from their childhood region already start to unlearn their local dialect long before they move, start to speak as they do in the capital and on TV, and in the same way it's possible to question whether it was being an outsider that made me long to get away, or if it was this longing to get away that made me, for all in this world, not want to fit in. The first time I felt the world get bigger was when my parents divorced and my father got a house closer to the city together with his new wife, and I would borrow her old green pants and her pink plastic jewellery and discover how much freer I felt when I didn't have to fit in with the village. I saw how my father always fit like a wolf in a flowerbed in that village, and I didn't understand what he meant when he bent down and said it was important I understood that it wasn't my fault they got divorced, because to me it seemed more like a wrong that had finally been corrected. I was eight when they divorced and ten when he moved to another city three hours away, and my sister and I had to take the train back and forth every other weekend, and the train became another home for me, free from my mum, free from my dad, free from the houses, the gardens, and the fences, and all the ugly things that were yelled from behind them when no one else heard, just me and my sister and three hours where I got to be the grown-up who knew all the stations by heart, my book, my Walkman, a handful of cassettes, and Leonard Cohen who sang in my headphones about first taking Manhattan and then taking Berlin, and I started going into the city alone, sat on the bus gazing into the necks of strangers and fell in love with the idea of who they might be, and I found new homes in the record stores and in the music library where I drifted around for hours, took the bus back home with my bag full of CDs and LPs which I would copy onto my cassettes, and I imagined how the buses fell in love too as they edged past each other in the dark, and the brakes sighed and the lights crackled like cellophane, and I leaned against the cold window, into shoegaze, white noise, and distorted guitars, and Sonic Youth sang *Teenage Riot*, and My Bloody Valentine sang *Sueisfine* which sounded like suicide, and I became increasingly aware that the world around me only functioned in bits and pieces, and I would have to put them together anew if everything was going to work. Cinema became another home away from home where the lights crackled, and Kieslowski taught me about liberty, equality, and fraternity, and in front of the TV I sat up night after night with the same grainy VHS copy of *My Own Private Idaho* and shed the same tears every time Keanu explained to River how he only had sex with guys for money, and besides, two guys can't love each other, and River replied that he could totally love someone even if he wasn't paid for it, because he loved Keanu and he didn't pay him, and every time River woke up, alone and abandoned on an empty back road, I found a home with him because my heart was there with him on that road, with River who was a Romeo too and dead long before I first saw the film. Later I found new homes with Gregg Araki who wrapped his films in blankets of shoegaze, white noise, and distorted guitars, and with Bruce LaBruce when I saw *The Raspberry Reich* on one of my first trips to Berlin, and the actors up on the screen were banging away in their best Baader-Meinhof gear while chanting together that there'd be no revolution without sexual revolution, and that there'd be no sexual revolution without homosexual revolution, and I left the cinema in ecstasy that I'd found other ways to give the world the finger than to pass out alone and abandoned on an empty back road. I enrolled in Film and Media Studies at the University in Copenhagen but had no idea what to answer when my grandfather asked what I'd become from studying that, since I hadn't yet realized it's possible to just lean into life and go along without having to become anything, that you can be a porn star one day and sell your body to a call centre the next and still make ends meet, that you can write a book and have people call you a writer and still not become anything because of it. After I dropped out of University, I lay one Christmas night in San Francisco, high on coke and poppers, and told the pink-haired punk who was my boyfriend at the time how my biggest fear was to fall through and land somewhere outside of life where I'd never make it up again, and he told me about the time a friend got him to buy coke from a street dealer, and when he complained to the dealer that it didn't look like coke he got knocked down and woke up the next day in hospital and owed $6,000 he didn't have, and compared to how easy it is to end up on the ground over there in what they like to call the land of opportunity, I never really fell myself, just made myself limp and floated away from any place of becoming, but all this still lay way ahead in the future, after I got my high school diploma and the next day packed everything I owned into a van while Belle & Sebastian sang about *Too Much Love* because, as it's always been whenever I moved, my stereo was the last thing I took down and the first thing I put up, in my new room, in the set of concrete blocks that were generally referred to, deadpan and with no trace of romance, as the Suicide Dorms.

I just asked my boyfriend to go to the Turkish market by the canal with me, but when I lift up my backpack, I can tell that Seahorse is still in there from last weekend. I can't take him out while my boyfriend is watching, but I also can't carry a four-pound silicone dick around on my back as we go shopping together; bananas, Boskoop apples, home-made ravioli, and those fresh green olives we both like so much. When I ordered Seahorse online I first thought of him as a Christmas present for myself, but I'd needed to borrow my boyfriend's credit card to complete the transaction, and when I asked to borrow the card, I of course said he was a present for the both of us. I also meant it when I said it, but the more filth I've dragged that beast through, the more he's become associated with a world that simply doesn't have room for my boyfriend too. Fortunately, my boyfriend needs to pee before we can go, so I quickly manage to put Seahorse back in his drawer. There's still dried-up lube like cobweb all along the shaft, along with all sorts of dirt from the backpack, so I better make sure to give him a good bath before I take him anywhere again.

I finally have plans to meet with Vincent again. I plan my whole day around this, have only cornflakes for breakfast since they move through faster, do a first line of speed in the afternoon to suppress hunger and speed up digestion, and when I clean out at around seven, I have a good feeling that I managed to get everything out and won't have to worry about it later, and when I sit on the bus and Lana Del Rey sings in my ears about being a waitress in a white dress listening to White Stripes, I'm just so damn proud of my butt hole, it feels like a tiny little sun I'm sitting on, and I tell myself that this is why I can feel spring leafing out in my stomach. He opens the door butt naked, opens it slightly and says he isn't done in the bathroom yet. He tells me just to chill, so I go to his room and see the pipe lying ready on his desk, see Tina ready on his desk, and I think I might as well get started, throw off my clothes and start sucking on the crystal fog, bend over forwards and let Tina blow hot air up my butt, expand my chest and widen my hips, and when he's finally done in the bathroom and pushes me down on the sofa, I'm so ready to explode like a supernova (to collapse around myself and turn into new stars) that a single hand feels like a dud, the way a small dick would back when dick-size still made a difference. We switch, I open up his rings, and sink into his core that yields like soft butter, I tighten my fist to make it wider and give him that feeling of death and resurrection I longed for before, but also to push him faster over the edge so it'll be my turn again, and when it is, I keep pushing backwards toward his free hand every time I feel it brush against my butt or the back of my thigh, and I hope he'll think of shoving it in next to the other one himself, that I won't have to ask for it, but he just keeps punching away in my helium core till he's tired out and we crash down on his sofa next to each other. He tells his phone to wake us in ten minutes, and because his body is used to Tina in a way mine is not, he's actually able to close his eyes and sink further down into something that looks a bit like sleep, and stay down there no matter how hard I cling to him and no matter how fast my moans stumble over each other while my butt hole howls like a washing machine set to spin on an empty stomach. When the ten minutes are over, we stay on our phones because we probably share the feeling now that our own hands aren't enough to satisfy each other's hunger right now, and he shows me a picture of the Ukrainian skinhead and asks if I know him, if I want him to come over, and I just say yes to everything, and we get up and walk together to the pipe and stand there for a bit blowing crystals down each other's lungs, but we're no longer horny for each other, not now there's a third one coming, so instead I take out Seahorse, shove him up my own butt, take a picture with my phone and send it to the Ukrainian skinhead with a message that I'm excited to see him. It's gonna be a while before he's here, so I stay on the bed with Seahorse up my butt while he's on the phone with the Ukrainian skinhead to figure out how long it'll be, and I find a smaller dildo and try to push it in next to Seahorse, but even though my will knows no limits, my sphincter refuses to open the last bit, so I look up at him and plead for help, and he puts down his phone, but instead of pushing the small dildo in next to Seahorse, he pulls out Seahorse, grabs the small dildo and pushes both hand and dildo inside, pulls out his hand and leaves the entire dildo in there behind my sphincter. I can tell right away that something isn't right in there, try to get the dildo out, but it's lodged sideways, and even though the base is only half a finger inside, it feels hopelessly stuck in its place, and I tell him to get it out right away but he also can't, no matter how hard I push my hips backwards towards him, and I can tell he's getting scared and is of no use now because all that matters now is to get the beast out, by all means necessary, and for all in this world avoid the emergency room. I grab a spoon and a fork from the kitchen and get to work in the bathroom, get down on my knees on the white tiled floor, bend over forward and push my hips back while I try to dig the spoon behind the base of the dildo so I can twist it towards the opening, but it's still stuck in its place, and he tells me to stop since it's started bleeding now, though only just a few drops, a soft pink hue to the clear mucous, and fortunately, the crystals prevent me from feeling any pain, just a blind determination to get the beast out, by all means necessary, so I keep my asshole open with my fingers, dig the fork into the dildo and try to pull it out this way, but the teeth of the fork just gnaw through the dildo's flesh and hack into my mucous membranes that yield like soft butter, and it's dripping dark red onto the white tiles now, and he tells me again to stop, but fortunately the crystals prevent me from feeling any pain, so I try again, and I also try with a nail file, but it doesn't make it better so I ask if he's got pliers, and he fetches a toolbox and tells me to stop while he hands me the pliers, and I dig in the pliers and bite down, and I can feel that they're missing their mark (that I'm not completely unable to feel pain after all), I finally manage to get a hold of the beast and yank at it hard, but just like the fork, the pliers gnaw through and hack into my mucous membranes that yield like soft butter, and I have to face that I'll never get the beast out on my own, and that there's no way around the emergency room. As we ring the bell for the night entrance I'm reduced to the world's most tired old gay joke, but I swallow it down, have no choice if I want to get the beast out, so I tell the scrubs that I know it's embarrassing before I tell them what happened, but they just nod like it's the most common thing in the world, as if I just fell on my bike or slipped in the bathroom and not on the world's biggest gay banana peel, and they tell me to follow them, just me alone, he unfortunately can't come (I hope it won't take more than an hour so we still have time to continue afterwards) and then I'm taken to a room with a bed waiting, I'm told to take off my clothes and I empty my pants of the toilet paper I stuffed between my butt cheeks so I wouldn't bleed all over everything on the way here, I'm handed a long white shirt that's open at the back, lay face down on the bed with my phone in my hand and write a message to the Ukrainian skinhead (to say I hope he's still free later so we can continue), and while the scrubs are away, I try to make sexy hospital selfies, let my shirt slip open and hold the phone in front of me so my butt cheeks stick up over my shoulder, and when the scrubs come back, I send a picture to the Ukrainian skinhead who replies that I'm mad, and even though it feels like I've got everything under control, it still makes me a little nervous since deep down I do remember that my usual sober self tries to stay away from the Ukrainian skinhead since my usual sober self actually believes that he's the one who's absolutely barking bonkers mad. I say I have to pee and am allowed to go to the bathroom, but nothing comes out no matter how hard it keeps pressing on my bladder, I say it's probably the dildo pressing against my prostate, and I say I'll try once more and see that there are bloodstains all the way from my room down to the toilet, but no matter how many times I try it still doesn't work, and then the scrubs come in with a pair of forceps and tell me to roll over on my side, and they try to get the beast out like this and say I should tell them if it hurts, but I don't feel anything, and they ask if I've been doing drugs, and I say that I've done a bit of speed because even though I quickly got used to being the world's biggest gay banana peel, I still can't admit to anything that has to do with Tina. The scrubs say there's no way around full anaesthesia, so I have to hand over my phone, and then we roll on to another room where they give me a saline drip and tranquillizer injections to get my pulse down to a place where the anaesthesia has a chance, and I tell them that even though I'm not able to pee, my bladder feels like it's about to burst, and I'm afraid I'm gonna piss all over everything as soon as they pull out the beast, but they just nod as if that's perfectly normal and ask me to sign that I might never wake up again though it's very unlikely, and then they're ready to start the anaesthesia, they say that if they can't get it out the way it came in, they'll have to cut open my stomach to get it out like that, but this is also very unlikely, so I just nod and try to talk about something else, and I keep on talking with no idea what I'm saying, and suddenly one of the scrubs asks if I'm aware it's all over. I look up at the clock and see that an hour has vanished, it's half past four in the morning, and the scrubs say I'll be discharged after rounds at ten, that I should try to get some sleep, but my first thought is to get my hands on my phone again, and as we roll on to the room where I'm supposed to get some sleep, I message the Ukrainian skinhead and ask if he's still up for something as soon as I'm discharged, and I ask if I can have a sleeping pill, but the scrubs says that after the anaesthesia this won't be necessary, I just need to lay down and under no circumstances try to get up, and if I need to pee, I'm gonna have to do it in the plastic bottle next to my bed, and I try again because my bladder is still about to burst, but it still doesn't work, and I know I'll never be able to sleep with this kind of pressure on my bladder, and besides, there are still the crystals in my blood that I haven't told them about, that still make me horny as fuck, and I start messaging whoever's online and tell them what happened, that I'm lying in the hospital and horny as fuck, that I hope it's fine for me to get fucked as soon as I'm discharged even though I'm sure it's gonna bleed like fuck, and I tell them I'm looking for people who'll fuck the shit out of me and won't stop no matter how hard it bleeds, that my ultimate fantasy right now is being gang-banged the shit out of by one after another with their dicks covered in blood from my ass, and I'm getting a whole bunch of flame emojis back, but not a single serious offer to fuck me. I try to pee again, but it's not possible the way I'm sitting here with my urinary system all bundled up in my lap, so I put my feet down on the floor and lift myself up in the darkness while I hold on to the bed and hold the plastic bottle under my dick and imagine I'm a soaking wet shirt on a hanger that the water just pours from all by itself, but no matter how hard I try, my groin is still all knotted up, and my asshole starts hurting, but this just makes me hornier and long even harder to get fucked the shit out of, so I lie back down and type that my asshole is hurting, that I want to get fucked the shit out of by someone who won't stop no matter how hard it bleeds, and again I'm getting all these flame emojis back, not because they all want to fuck me, but because they're all sitting at home tugging their tiny worn-down penises while also dreaming of getting fucked the shit out of till it bleeds. I try to pee again, stand there with the plastic bottle under my dick and try to forget it's there, try to forget about my body there in the dark so gravity can just do its thing and make it flow, but then the door opens and one of the scrubs enters with her back full of sharp blinding lights, she hisses that I'm not allowed to stand up, paces back and forth like she's trying to work out how to drive me back into bed without getting near me, and I realize that my shirt has slipped off my body, that I'm standing there all naked in front of her, but right now there's nothing more important in the world than emptying this damn cursed bladder, so I just say I'm sorry, say I'm holding onto the bed so nothing's gonna happen, and she finally gives up and walks away, leaving me to stand alone there in the dark till time almost comes to a halt, and I finally hear a quiet drumming at the bottom of the bottle. The breakfast cart comes around, and nothing of course has been ordered for me, but I don't want anything either, I tell them I'll be discharged at ten and prefer to eat at home, though I have no intention of going home or eating when I'm discharged; it's been more than twenty-four hours since I last ate anything, and my plan is still to get fucked the shit out of for the rest of the day without having to worry about my digestion, but then my boyfriend texts me because apparently I somehow posted a picture of Seahorse and myself, the kind of post Instagram's private vice squad should have been on guard to strike down, with Coca Cola and bloodshot eyes, because it definitely violated every community guideline, but apparently some things do slip through, and even though my boyfriend is okay with me fucking around, he's not okay with me posting pictures while I do it, and I obviously know this and do think it's totally fair, but also, tonight was no sort of ordinary night, and I try to explain this without letting him know what happened, I just tell him it's been the worst date I ever experienced, and he asks why I don't just come home, and I tell him it isn't possible, but he doesn't understand this, so I tell him I'll explain when I come home, but apparently I made it sound more dramatic than it is because he asks if I'm locked up somewhere, if he needs to come and get me, he does have work to go to, but if it's an emergency of course he'll come, and I assure him it's all under control, but he's worried now and wants to come and get me anyway, and so I explain that I'm at the hospital, but that I'm okay, that it's nothing serious, just stupid and silly, and right now I'm just waiting to be discharged, and I'll explain it all when he gets home from work. Times moves on, it becomes ten, and I can't be in this room anymore, it becomes eleven, and I can't be in this body anymore, not in this room anymore, because I'm not high anymore, just a body around a wound that wants to stay open regardless of what I want myself anymore, it becomes twelve, it becomes one, and I tell the scrubs I can't take it anymore, and they say the doctor's gonna be there any moment now, but still it becomes two, and I gather my things and drag myself out of there since no matter what they say, I can't for one moment anymore, but as soon as I'm out on the street, my energy returns, not exactly lust, but at least the ability to put one foot in front of the other and obey the wound that won't stop bleeding between them. When he lets me back inside his flat, thirteen hours have passed since we went together to the emergency room, and he says he mostly just slept a bit and otherwise fucked himself with Seahorse and messaged a couple of guys who promised they'd come over but never showed, and he asks if I still think I'm able to continue, and I pause, because no matter how hard my butt hole longs to get fucked, a fist is probably still stretching it, but I can't leave without charging my blood with fresh crystals from his desk, and even though it's not exactly lust that fills me, it does increase my body's need to bleed, I imagine lying on all fours in Tiergarten with a circle of blood-smeared dicks rubbing cum into my wound, but when I soon after find myself in Tiergarten the bushes are still too barren to hide anything, at least as long as the sun is high in the sky, and the men who look like they hoped to do hidden things in the bushes don't look like the kind that would be into sharing a bleeding wound, at least not as long as the sun is high in the sky, so I walk away from there, down through Schöneberg with black metal in my ears and my gaze buried in my phone while I throw flame emojis at anyone around me who looks like they might be into sharing a bleeding wound. I'm interrupted when my boyfriend calls because I didn't see his messages, and he's worried now because I didn't text him after I was discharged (which also, technically, I never was), and also he's worried because I still never told him what I was doing in the hospital, and I apologise for being so lost inside my own head, but I also can't say it out loud out here on the street, and I promise again that I'll explain it all when he's home from work, but then he figures it out by himself and is angry I didn't just tell him the truth from the start, and I use my anaesthesia as an excuse and say I'm on my way home now, he tells me to get some sleep and not do any more drugs, and I'm shocked that he thinks I would actually do this, even though it's exactly what I intend to do, and I try to soothe him and tell him I love him (which is true), even though I'm also glad I still have seven hours before he gets home from work. I sit down against a tree in the middle of a roundabout buzzing with warm orange evening sun while I continue throwing flame emojis at guys I usually wouldn't touch with a ten-foot pole, but still nothing happens, so I text a friend who I know collects bleeding wounds like they were stamps, who loves to trade and pass on, and I describe my wound and how I got it, ask him what he thinks my chances are of finding someone who'll fuck me and not stop no matter how hard it bleeds, and even though I say I'm asking for a friend, I'm expecting him to have me over and fuck me, but instead he replies that it sounds like a super bad idea if I don't want permanent damage, and the let-down sends me crashing to the ground, and I almost message the Ukrainian skinhead and ask if maybe he'd just be up for cuddling for a bit, just give me a hug, but then I think it's probably best that I go home and get some sleep like my boyfriend said I should. Though of course I can't sleep when I get home, I lie down on the sofa and see that Angelito has texted me since apparently he was the first person I messaged this morning after I woke from the anaesthesia and really wanted to see someone, and I explain it all to him, how horny and alone I've been, and he asks me how I'm doing and if I still want to see him, because he was taking drugs with some friends and really wants to fuck me now, and I reply that I want it, and I reply that I want it to hurt, but I warn him that it probably won't be possible without it starting to bleed, and even though I'm totally fine with this, I also understand if he's not, and to my big surprise he just tells me to come over. Angelito welcomes me in his thong as usual, I give him a tight squeeze, and he smiles in surprise as usual, our lips melt together, and I already feel the half ecstasy I swallowed on my way here, or maybe it's just my feverish need to feel him, and I pull the waistband down over his perfectly rounded butt cheeks, say yes when he offers me mephedrone and G, spread my legs over the towels on his stained sofa, and almost cry with happiness when he puts his dick inside me and starts fucking me like a horny school boy and when he stops in-between to wipe away the blood, he tells me it's really not that bad and then goes on while I look up with pleading eyes at this divine creature who's fucking me, a blonde little cherub who looks down from Michelangelo's heaven and whispers they just filled the candy bowl up there, and as he's just about to cum, our mouths fall open and we sink as deep into each other's eyes as we can get, and when he finally shoots inside me, I whisper *thank you, thank you, thank you* and have never felt this close to saying I love him, even though I also know it's about something completely different.

It's about running away together and moving together into a house that's already on fire.

A problem when writing about love is that it's hard to say what the word even means, besides that love is the feeling we feel when we love, because even though Romeo never doubts that he loves Juliet, there are others who simply love pizza or techno, and in this way, the word quickly loses all meaning. As a nineteen-year-old, I gave up becoming a writer since I didn't believe that I'd ever be able to express with words how big it was to have your heart broken. Today it seems silly, but back then, nothing could have mattered more, and if I couldn't describe how unfair it felt to sit there with all this love that nobody wanted, it seemed pointless to try and write at all. Better just to pick from the words that had already been written, like when my sister and I watched *Romeo + Juliet* together, and Leonardo DiCaprio yelled at a clear blue sky that the stars could go fuck themselves, or when Stuart Murdoch from Belle & Sebastian sang that he just wanted to dance and drink whiskey and go off to town, and he sang that it was because the snow was falling, because the snow was falling, and he kept repeating this until the song was over, that it was because the snow was falling, and I wrote down the words in the margins of my day planner since I didn't believe I'd ever be able to say it better myself. There are books I keep around for the love I can find in a single sentence, just for the comfort of having them on my shelf among all the others. Such a book is Inger Christensen's *Alphabet,* which I sometimes take out just to read the first sentence, just to read that the apricot trees exist, so simple and yet so grave that she has to repeat it, that the apricot trees exist, and William Burroughs' diaries, where on the final page, three days before his death from a heart attack, he asks himself what love is, and he answers himself that love is the most natural painkiller, and when I flip forward though Inger Christensen's poems where, with each letter, the world accelerates further into perplexing complexity, or when I dive back into William Burroughs' life as a homosexual junkie and literary outlaw, those two sentences are always with me, like a hug I can always reach out for, like a home I can always return to. In her book *All About Love*, bell hooks searches for a sentence that truly says all there is to say about love, and she picks one from Scott Peck's self-help book *The Road Less Travelled* that says love is the will to extend yourself for the purpose of nurturing your own or someone else's spiritual growth, not because this best says what we usually mean when we talk about love, but because it's this understanding bell hooks wants to pass on in her own book. My boyfriend bought it as a Christmas present for his sister after several people recommended it, he started sneak reading before giving it to her and thought I might have a few things to learn from it too, and though I didn't particularly expect to like it since it seemed pointless to me to impose such a positive definition onto something I knew could be both ugly and destructive, I did see that if this will to extend myself wasn't necessarily an exhaustive definition, but rather an ideal for how to live out love in practice, there might be a few good points to take from the book, and also there was something fitting about how reading it on my boyfriend's recommendation (he who I've always known is the better person between us, he who gets out his wallet every time we meet a homeless person in the U-Bahn, he who tries to help transgender inmates in German prisons while I literally just sit here writing about my own asshole) in itself felt like an effort to extend myself for the purpose of both mine and his spiritual growth. The book still lies on the shelf beneath our coffee table with two bookmarks in it because even though our reasons were different, neither of us could be bothered reading it to the end, and he ended up buying a different present for his sister, and actually this turned out to be a good thing since his sister had also already read it after it was recommended to her, and she didn't like it either, and in this way it's become something we have together, we can all wonder together why all these people go around recommending this book. My boyfriend's biggest problem was the lack of concrete advice; it didn't get much closer than saying you don't nurture someone's spiritual growth by hitting them, and this we probably could've figured out on our own. I lost patience after reading several times that parents who hit their children, by definition, can't love them, because even though I never got hit as a child, I do know many who grew up in families where handing out a slap as a final resort was not unheard of, and though this does sound wrong to me, the biggest difference I find between them and myself is not how much we feel we were loved, but how serious we feel it is to have been hit, and even though I do see it as a flaw to be able to hit one's own child,

I also know that just a few generations ago, this was simply common practice, that back then there was no option but to send one's children to a school where slapping and caning were part of everyday life, and I refuse to believe that back then no one loved their children, and even though I do see it as a flaw to be able to hit one's own child, and though I do believe this to be a flaw that can be passed down by hitting, I refuse to accept an idea that says the flaws we carry with us and pass on without wanting to, mean that we aren't capable of love. When my own need to write about love only appeared after I'd been dumped, it's probably because my idea of love was so wound up in classic tales of impossible lovers that love just seemed bigger and more important the more got in the way. The prime example is Shakespeare's play about Romeo and Juliet, though Shakespeare's Romeo could not have been the same without Pyramus and Tristan and many other Romeos before him, and actually Shakespeare's idea of love is pretty problematic as well because in the balcony scene where Romeo climbs up to declare his love for Juliet, Juliet actually tells Romeo several times to get down from her balcony, but Romeo is raised to believe that love is something he'll always have to fight for, and to Romeo, a no is never just a no but a challenge to overcome, and it doesn't make it better that Juliet in the play is only thirteen and Romeo around sixteen, and in this way, it's not even quite legal what he's up to, and when you bear in mind that Romeo, when he climbs up to Juliet's balcony, had only seen her once before at a party and never even spoke with her, and that the very same morning he was crying his heart out over some other girl, then Romeo quickly starts to appear like a bit of a fuckboy, like someone who's probably more smitten with his own big feelings, with drama for drama's sake, than with anything that's specifically about Juliet. Nevertheless, I clearly saw myself in Romeo's struggles to have his love recognised, and so I spent a long time collecting ideas for my own Romeo story, a novel in which my Romeo character would both work as an alter ego, an attempt to distance myself from my own defeats, and at the same time embody the very primordial myth of the hopeless love that I myself was so very hopelessly in love with. The novel I gave up writing was planned as an endless series of failures where Romeo is dumped over and over again, and most of the chapters would end with him being seduced by his gym teacher, a pizza guy, or a random construction worker while slowly becoming so hardened by the repetition and the lack of meaning that he completely loses the ability to feel anything, which for Romeo is a greater tragedy than getting dumped, because as long as he was only dumped, at least he still had his love to understand himself by. A Romeo is a Romeo is a Romeo, but no matter by what name we call him, it won't make him any less of a Romeo. A small scented twink with no concept of what he wants and still a burning desire to die for it. He who goes by many names but, whether he drinks poison or goes down with the Titanic, in the end is always the same Romeo. And since I was a teenager in the nineties, my Romeo will always have the body and face of a young Leonardo DiCaprio, who played him in Baz Luhrmann's *Romeo + Juliet* from 1996. I'd already seen him as Jim Carroll in *The Basketball Diaries* and Arthur Rimbaud in *Total Eclipse*, both films where he incorporated agony and made it sexy the way only Leo could, and the more his little baby face was covered in tears, snot, and saliva, the more he howled hysterically and shivered from withdrawal, the more he stood for me as the epitome of ultimate longing and everything I could ever want to long for myself. My ultimate Romeo moment is still the scene in *Romeo + Juliet* where Leo yells at a clear blue sky that the stars can go fuck themselves. It happens after he's been banished and exiled to Mantua (a small town in Lombardy where Monteverdi in 1607 premiered his opera about Orpheus, another one of the big proto-Romeos), and here Romeo now sits in a trailer on a scorched field among barren sheep and waits for news from Verona, and when his friend shows up and tells him that Juliet is dead, Leo falls to his knees and yells up at the empty blue sky, with his unbuttoned Hawaiian shirt fluttering in the wind, that the stars can go fuck themselves, and even though it's tragic, there's something pathetic about it too, because Juliet is not really dead, and even though Romeo doesn't know this yet, the audience knows, and Romeo only exists through the gaze of the audience, and therefore he does know that this is his moment to shine, that the love we all came to admire will never appear stronger or purer than now. Romeo loves, and therefore he is, but when some love pizza, others techno, what does it even make sense to say about love. bell hooks sees love as an action, not a feeling, but Romeo just wants to feel as much as humanly possible, so much that everything else loses its meaning. In a battle between bell hooks and Romeo, I'd be #teamromeo all the way since my entire idea of love is created in Romeo's image, and though he might come across as a bit of a cry-baby next to the American professor, he'll still be my personal champion no matter how hard he loses, and even though I'd wish for a page in my own book where love would wait as pure and edifying as it does in Inger Christensen's apricot trees or in William Burroughs' painkillers, a place where it's all just about me and my boyfriend's spiritual growth, in my mind, all roads lead to Romeo, and when I say Romeo, I mostly mean myself and my own Romeo complex, because whether I like it or not, Romeo will always be part of me, and in the end, this is how Romeo works, that nothing is more important to Romeo than being a Romeo, and in this way Romeo can never really lose, because the more Romeo loses, the more Romeo he becomes.

First time my heart was broken for real was by Alexander. He was my high school boyfriend, my first real Romeo, and the first one to just stand by as I slowly got obsessed. Alexander had shiny dark hair and huge brown eyes that gave a feeling of depth when you looked into them. He had big juicy lips always freshly hydrated with the tiny Blistex jar he carried around in his pocket, and when he walked his bike through the pedestrian street, it was always with his head slightly tilted, as if he was prepared for anyone walking past to give him a smack on the head. First time I saw Alexander was in the youth group at the local gay and lesbian centre in an old bike cellar somewhere in the city. From the age of fifteen I'd been sitting there every other Thursday, drinking bitter coffee and hoping that someone would stop by I could imagine being boyfriends with, and over time I'd become the one with the key who had to arrive half an hour early to make the coffee and wait, but still I couldn't imagine being boyfriends with any of the ones that showed up, not until Alexander suddenly sat there on the sofa across from me with his hands clasped between his knees and bowed gratefully as I poured him his coffee. My first thought was that he looked like Romeo's friend in the movie with Leonardo DiCaprio, the one who shows up in Mantua and tells Romeo that Juliet is dead because besides my Romeo complex I'd long held a soft spot for Romeo's friend, who watches over Leo with the biggest brownest eyes I could possibly imagine, and every time Leo fell to his knees with his Hawaiian shirt fluttering in the wind and yelled at the bright blue sky that the stars could go fuck themselves, my thoughts went to his friend in the background, how he should at least run over and offer his Romeo a hug (a body for his grief to lean on), and I thought if I were Romeo in this movie, I'd forget about the girl once I had the brown-eyed's arms around me. Alexander said he went to the same school as me, that we'd been in the same year for more than a year now, and as I sat there trying to comprehend how I could've overlooked those eyes for so long, a quite fantastical thing happened when a wind blew in through the bike cellar, grabbed hold of us both, and lifted us up through the ceiling, up through the five floors above us, carried us into a sky that was full of stars, violins, and trumpets, flung us far into each other, into a union that wasn't a kiss and wasn't sex but felt like so much more, and the fact that all of this only happened inside my head didn't mean it didn't happen, it just meant that when we afterward sat in the bike cellar across from each other, there was no way for me to tell if he'd felt it too, and this was all I could focus on for the rest of the night (had he felt it, or was it just me?), no matter how hard I tried to take part in the conversation and not act like I'd just been shot through the heart by some little chubby cartoon angel. A few months went by where we just said hi when we passed each other in the school yard and chatted about hair wax and shoes, and I learnt that an arrow through the heart can feel like a knife when I heard Alexander had kissed another guy from the youth group, someone I definitely couldn't imagine being boyfriends with, though it helped when I sensed how important it was for Alexander to let me know that he couldn't either. First time I kissed Alexander was after a movie night at my house. I was home alone and only invited him and his friend Nanna, who had frizzy red hair and always wore the same red raincoat the colour of heart-shaped stickers and roses. I don't remember what films we saw first, but since it was at my house, John Waters' *Cry Baby* and Gus Van Sant's *My Own Private Idaho* are good guesses, though the latter might have been a bit dark for a night when I hoped for love to finally find its way to the village. Alexander and I were both shy so Nanna had to steer the conversation, she asked how it could be that girls didn't worry about HIV anymore, and I replied that it was probably because they had a much bigger risk of getting pregnant, and if you walk along a road where you can easily get hit by a car, you probably don't think much about how a plane can still come crashing down and hit you on the head. After the second movie, Nanna said she had to leave even though it was past midnight and the last bus had already left, but she had a friend in a village four kilometres away and had planned already to sleep at her place. It was early December and just below zero, and it was raining earlier in the evening, so there'd definitely be ice on the roads, and even with the woollen sweater under it, the raincoat didn't seem nearly warm enough, but Nanna insisted, and Alexander didn't say anything, so I figured it was something they'd planned between them. Be careful you don't get hit by a plane, she said as she waved goodbye in the driveway. Afterwards we saw *Hannibal & Jerry* in my sister's bed, we cuddled her stuffed animals and planted kisses on each other's faces with their hard little plastic noses, and it became more and more obvious that what we really wanted was to do it with our own lips, and yet it took most of the film before we finally got there, and here I'm gonna skip what happened next because neither of us was very good at it yet, and even though I never questioned my love, my sexuality hadn't become part of me yet; my wildest fantasies were still about kissing a guy at a party, holding hands on the bus on the way home, comparing hopes and dreams on a sofa in the morning sun, whereas taking each other's clothes off and rubbing out orgasms for each other seemed more like a chore, like a blob of ink that had to be put on paper to confirm the vows of the kisses that, in the end, were all that really mattered. Then came the Christmas party at our school where Alexander dressed up like a Gaultier advertisement with a striped sailor blouse, glitter sparkling all over his face, and a white sailor hat tilted to the side while he held his head high, and we kissed and pretended not to notice everyone staring, not before they yelled cool and congratulations and showered us with hugs and confetti, and we went together to the Psyched Up Janis concert where they recorded their acoustic live album, and we sat in the fourth row and kept on kissing through the entire show (passing back and forth the glitter and confetti that lived on our skin now), and we went together to his friend's birthday party in a community centre somewhere in the suburbs, where we drank ourselves silly on vodka and anything carbonated, and then back home in his bed where I sucked his dick while Air sang that all I need's a little time, and we woke up, and he said he was happy because he'd been so drunk that he'd finally just been able to relax and not worry about if he enjoyed it the right way, and he put on his Erasure CD and sang along to *A Little Respect*, and he put on his Saint Etienne CD and sang along to *Sylvie* and said that the opening line, *seventeen, high school queen*, was definitely about him. On the day in April when Alexander broke up with me, I covered a whole page in my day planner with white-out and wrote, *cry my eyes out over Alexander*, with letters so small you could cut yourself on them, but this didn't hold back the spring, and it didn't stop the sun from staying up longer each day until it was finally summer, and I got a new boyfriend with orange freckles, yellow spikes, and a black belt in karate who everyone said was hot, and everyone was jealous over, and everyone sucked off behind my back when we went out together, but it didn't really bother me since I was a Romeo, wanted back my Romeo, and couldn't bear that life went on without him. It was no surprise that I took it this way because a year before Alexander, there'd been another Alexander who appeared like another Romeo on a Saturday night at a party in the bike cellar, twenty minutes before they closed, with big juicy lips and huge brown eyes that gave a feeling of depth when you looked into them, and we walked each other to the night bus and parted with a kiss that promised way more than it ever intended to keep, and after this night, I spent a year feeling heartbroken over the Alexander I'd only known for twenty minutes, until the next Alexander came along and broke my heart for real. I already had a hunch that Alexander was cooling off before he broke up with me, but I wrote it off as late-winter blues, and on top of that there was the flu that kept us apart an entire week before I left on a school trip to Rome, and even though it was him who broke up with me, I eagerly accepted all the blame and thought, as I have thought so many times since then, that had I just been better at showing my love and the extent of it, he couldn't possibly have walked away from it. That was until that day during break when Nanna told me a thing that was supposed to be a secret because Alexander still seemed confused about it, which was that he started seeing a girl after me, and it'd be years before I could smile about how it always made me think of *Strange Attraction* by The Cure where the girlfriend whispers, can I use some of your lipstick, because when Nanna told me, the light just went out inside me, and everything went cold because the love I'd understood myself by had maybe never been real to him, just an experiment, a performance he had to numb himself with vodka to really believe. As long as I was still in Rome, Alexander was still my Romeo, and I loved how history rustled everywhere around me, how all these stories of greatness and fall only made the love I was heading home to prove seem even grander. But with great expectations come great disappointments, and after a three-hour bus ride to Pompeii I just wanted more contorted faces trapped in lava, and after our three hours slouch around the Vatican I wanted more than just a painted sky to look up at like fish in a barrel while everyone snapped away with disposable cameras and ignored the speakers telling us to be quiet in five different languages. I'd rather just lie in the grass on the Palatine Hill where the ruins were less famous and the air was herbal sweet, a mix of mint and lemon balm that hovered everywhere though we never found the actual plants. At the hotel, we mixed drinks in our toothbrush cups and smoked filterless cigarettes from a soft orange pack, we lounged out on big, wide marble stairs and did our best to ignore the street vendors, their long-stemmed roses, and all their notions about who should buy them for who, because once you made eye contact, they were impossible to shake, and I thought of Alexander and the love I still believed would conquer everything, while at the same time just wallowing in the image of myself lounged out on the biggest, widest marble stairs under the sun, puffing away on filterless cigarettes till the pack was empty. The night I came back, I'd planned to meet with Alexander in front of the station. It was chilly and drizzling a bit, but it didn't matter since summer was coming, and I bought him the same Italian football shirt I also got for myself so we could lope into summer together and show the world how we belonged together, and we'd be off for somebody's birthday together, but instead, he just said he didn't think we should be boyfriends anymore; he said it just didn't feel right anymore and therefore wasn't fair to me either. I felt like I just dropped a rare and expensive vase on the floor, but a vase that was filled with all of my hopes and dreams, and though I didn't mind carrying all the blame on my own, I didn't understand why we weren't already down on our knees together, picking up all the pieces together, helping each other glue them back together together, but this was of course because it wasn't actually a vase, only my hopes and dreams, and those need a lot more than just glue to put back together. My head was bursting with a longing to cry so he'd at least be able to see how broken I was, but sadly, this is a flaw I've always had, that I've never been able to cry over things that happen in my own life, only things that happen on film, like when Leo dies with trembling lips, or when Keanu tells River in *My Own Private Idaho* that two guys can't love each other, but when I get hurt in real life, it just feels like an emptiness that goes all the way down through my body and continues down through the Earth, and the more I try to show the pain on my face by crying, the more it feels like a lie. I looked into his eyes and realized that the darkness there was also just a surface, that whatever I saw behind them only existed inside my own head, but I was too busy arranging the blame to let it properly sink in; I was still convinced that if I'd just told him properly how much I loved him, there's no way he could have done this to me.

It was in social studies Romeo first learnt about how unfair love can be. The students thought there should be enough love for everyone, that everyone should give and receive equally, but it wasn't so simple, the teacher said, this would make society come to a halt. A student put his hand up and said it's a pity for those who never receive anything. But the teacher said that a love no one asked for can be just as bad. A forest of hands went up, and the teacher already knew what they would say, that resources should be distributed equally. He tried a new strategy and asked if anyone in the classroom ever tried to love and give lots of love that no one accepted. All hands went down immediately. The teacher knew it was getting personal, but it was important for his lesson. Romeo slowly raised a hand. There was a giggle from the back row, but the teacher told them this was nothing to be embarrassed about. So, Romeo had given lots of love that no one accepted? Romeo nodded calmly. But then, what happened when no one accepted his love? Romeo mumbled something no one could hear, and the teacher asked him to speak up. He gave more love; he went all red in the face as he said it. And when did he run out of love? The question made the whole class laugh, even Romeo, because he never ran out of love. It doesn't work like that; the more love he gave, the more love he had to give, even if he never got anything back. The students went quiet. They didn't understand exactly how it all worked, but it was clear that the teacher had a point; a certain amount of inequality was necessary, and then they could pack up their social justice talk because if love was fair, it would wither and die.

It's been two days since I took off from the hospital and I finally managed to get a bit of sleep. After getting home from Angelito's I just lay awake all night with my eyes closed, had already taken ten of the strong melatonin tablets and pretended to be asleep when my boyfriend came in and lay down next to me, couldn't risk that he'd put his arm around me and feel how my cardiac system still fought over me, and as soon as he was asleep I got up again and swallowed ten more tablets and did so every other hour till I finally sank into a formless daze where my muscles and my thoughts started dissolving into something I was no longer in control of, though it wasn't until last night that I finally managed to let go completely. I wake up alone in our bedroom again, sweaty and sticky under a sour rag that used to be my blanket. There's a message on my phone from Vincent who's feeling guilty now and asks if I'm okay. I have no idea what to say to him, because the more sedatives I sweat out of my body, the more it feels like a carving knife I'm lying with between my thighs, but I'm also afraid to feel around down there, afraid to ruin even more down there than I already have, hardly dared to eat anything yet because I'm afraid of what'll happen when I eventually have to poop, so I just text him back and say I'll probably need a few weeks to recover and really hope that's all.

A Romeo is a Romeo is a Romeo, and no matter by what name we call him, he'll still smell as sticky-sweet of sunstroke and cheap deodorant. Romeo is standing at a motorway junction outside a suburb north of Rome. He's there with his Julian, with his thumb out, trying to hitch a ride back north. Their plan is to sleep on beaches and in lay-bys, draw straws over who's gonna suck off the next truck driver for a ride together. Romeo's skin glows like baby oil in the sun. It's all this symbolism he's been mired in. Romeo was built to get loaded up with romantic ideas, all the cheapest tricks in the book, all my wildest fantasies of death and destruction, and Romeo can carry it all since it's the promise of tragedy that him keeps him going, the story of poor little Romeo who's been *oh* so abandoned and now deserves a whole book to go on about how unfair it is.

Second time my heart was broken for real was by Julian. He was my first long-term relationship, if a year and a half counts as long-term, and if the breaks count as part of the relationship, and in our case I think they should since the breaks in our relationship were like the breaks that, according to Brian Eno, are just as important to the music as the notes. First time I saw Julian was at a communication workshop held by the Stop AIDS Campaign in Copenhagen, where I'd volunteered and was there to learn to talk to strangers about condoms and sex. It was the spring before I moved to Copenhagen, a new millennium had just begun, and Julian welcomed me with a smile like sandy beaches and eyes like the sun playing in the waves over the sea. It was before we knew that sex without a condom was no longer a suicide pact (at least not in Denmark, not like back in the eighties when a famous comedian said on TV that AIDS was a beautiful disease because you died from too much love), and Julian's smile was still just a photo on a pinboard, but light filled the windows and embraced everything with a warmth that made even the Stop AIDS pen in my hand glow with hope and expectations, and every time I passed by Julian on the pinboard I smiled back and was a little more blinded by my faith in the love I still depended on to conquer everything. A few weeks later, I was back in Copenhagen for another workshop, and this time Julian was there in person. I was already so sure that Julian and I were made for each other, that when we stood together at the Pan Club just before midnight, each with a pint of beer in our hands and made out, it felt like both the most miraculous and the most natural thing in the world. Julian said that he had keys to the campaign offices if I wanted to go back there where it was quieter, and I nodded timidly since I already knew where this was going, and he was two years older than me, so no doubt he knew what he was doing, but when we lay up there on the sofa together, with cartoon condoms and monochrome men in leather vests and aluminium frames looking down from all sides, and I tried to open the button on his jeans, he just pushed away my hand and said he'd rather wait, and though the kisses were still more important than whatever the undressing was expected to lead to, it hurt me a bit that our love wasn't limitless from the start, but it was also just a tiny chip which I fully relied on time to take care of. Then came my first summer in Copenhagen where all doors and windows were wide open, and since I'd learnt from the provinces that any opening was an opportunity that couldn't be wasted, the hunt for my next Romeo became pretty much a full-time occupation. There was Matteo from Italy who I could easily imagine being boyfriends with, there was Patrick from Malmö who already imagined he was boyfriends with me, there were all the guys in the bars, in the chat, and in the park, and when I, with one arm around Matteo or Patrick or one of the others, ran into Julian at the Pan Club again, it was hard to explain how it didn't make a difference whether it was one, the other, or a third, because a Romeo is a Romeo, and in the end I still believed that Julian was the Romeo that was meant for me, but this idea of a Romeo who can't have his Romeo, of a rose that grows but never reaches its sun, was outdated now, since having each other wasn't any harder than having a pizza on our way down Nørrebrogade, the only problem now was having to choose, so I chose Rasmus who I saw one night at the Pan Club, dancing to Britney Spears in his Rage Against The Machine T-shirt as the lights turned his strawberry curls pissy yellow, and meanwhile I just became still more convinced that Julian was my one true Romeo. I'm not sure when and where I finally kissed Julian again, maybe because it felt less like a resolution and more like a wrong that had finally been corrected, I just remember it was December, and we kept it a secret because Rasmus' friend, who I was studying for a TV history exam with, had promised to make my life hell if I didn't treat Rasmus well, and instead I just said to Rasmus, the way Alexander once said to me, that it just didn't feel right anymore. What I remember best from my first months with Julian is the time we spent in bed together, either in his studio flat in a suburb down South or in my dorm room on Amager, where the sleeper sofa was only eighty centimetres wide, and we took the mattress down on the floor so we could comfortably let our arms and legs lie outside as we spooned or I fucked him or he fucked me, and we'd lie afterwards and discuss whether we preferred being the one who fucked or the one who got fucked, and every time we'd agree that both were equally fantastic. After all this time when sex had been more about doing it than about how it felt when I did it, it felt like I finally got what it was about (or at least what it was about to me, at that time, with him), it was about the borders of our bodies opening up, the territories that used to be mine merging with the territories that used to be his so that the life inside us was free to roam wherever it pleased. For Christmas he gave me a jar of chocolate body paint, and I drew a heart on his stomach, licked it off and saved the rest for later, and then we started planning our summer together. His idea was to fly to Rome and hitch-hike back, sleep on beaches and in lay-bys, suck off truck drivers for the next ride, and it sounded both dangerous and romantic, like a world free of borders, and I just said yes to everything, but when spring came he started shutting down and rejecting my touches; there were barricades I couldn't cross, doors I couldn't open, closets with skeletons he hadn't put there himself but still had to put up with, and though I wish I could throw it all wide open here and not just cover it with pictures, there are still parts of this story that aren't mine to tell. The first time Julian broke up with me I spent a month on the floor, ate his body paint on crackers and felt just as shattered as my hopes and dreams, and when the jar was empty, I crawled back to Rasmus, hoping he would piece me back together, but of course the moment Rasmus had me back up on my feet, Julian came back and said we could be boyfriends again, fly to Rome and hitch-hike back, sleep on beaches and in lay-bys and all the other stuff we talked about, and so for the second time I had to let Rasmus down with no explanation except that it didn't feel right anymore. On our first night in Rome, we had pizza and walked around for hours with no concern where the streets would take us. I asked why it felt like we were walking around inside a film studio, was it the pleasant stillness or the orange crackle of the streetlights, was it the apricots that seemed too exotic to just lie there all over the pavement, or was it the sweetness that saturated the air so that breathing alone was enough to make you full. Since there were neither beaches nor lay-bys in Rome, we'd treated ourselves and rented a hotel room for the first week, but when I woke up in bed the morning after, it felt like I'd been kicked in the stomach by a horse, I couldn't get anything down at the breakfast buffet, and the cheeseburger I managed to eat at the station only made everything worse. We tried to walk to the Spanish Steps but every step I took just added pain to the pain, and Julian had to support me all the way back to our room where I could finally collapse back onto the bed and thrash around, whining and moaning as the pain continued to grow all by itself. Julian thought I should eat as lightly as possible so he went out for groceries and came back with white bread, white yoghurt, and vacuum-sealed white potatoes, and I ate a few spoons of the yoghurt and drank five litres of water, but my stomach didn't get better, and my world shrank down to my sticky bed sheets and the toilet where brown water squirted violently from my butt and made my asshole burn as if I'd shat a cactus. Julian tried to cheer me up, goofed around and put on puppet shows with the potatoes I couldn't eat anyway, but I couldn't forgive myself for ruining our adventure together, that our summer of no borders had ended up in unwilling isolation because of me, and after four days we took a taxi to a hospital where I got a saline drip and was told to stop eating completely and only drink water until I got better, and as the week came to an end, the pain finally subsided, but it felt like all strength and will had been flushed down the toilet, and instead of thumbing it, we took a train to the airport and from there, the first flight back to Denmark. Instead of sleeping on beaches and in lay-bys and all the other stuff we talked about, we got on the train to his mother's farm in Western Jutland, where we took long walks along golden yellow rape fields or stayed in the guest room on the mattress on the floor where I tried to compensate with kisses and caresses for all the truck drivers we never got to blow, until Julian got up and told me he was fed up with all my affirmation bullshit and didn't think we should be boyfriends anymore. I swept myself up in a garbage bag and sent it back to Amager where I'd eventually throw myself into a deep deep hole, but before I got that far, Julian decided it was okay for us to still be friends together, and he decided it was okay for us to still have sex together, and then I didn't mind so much that we weren't boyfriends anymore, and I wasn't so much bothered by whoever else he did it with because rarely had the borders been so free between us; doors and windows stood wide open, there was nowhere I wasn't allowed, and when he finally asked if we should be boyfriends again, I just nodded eagerly and felt certain that third time would be the charm. He took my hand as we walked down the high road together, started planning a second go at a summer of beaches, lay-bys, and truck drivers, and I took him to my grandfather's birthday and fucked him in the community centre toilets while he laughed and told me I had to be quieter if I didn't want my entire family to hear us, and I was so blinded by my faith in love's final victory that it took me a long time before I noticed when the borders tightened again, but slowly I did start to see it, a pattern in our relationship that was as predictable as the narrative structure of fairy tales, a studied choreography we repeated over and over again; we started completely tangled up in each other, then he would slowly push me away and turn from me till he completely shoved me aside, and from there, he reached out towards me again, let me take his hand and pulled me closer till he held me tightly again and whispered in my ear that he was ready to take me back. Each stage of the choreography served a purpose; it was like the music where the pauses are just as important as the notes, and therefore I didn't get how different rules would apply to the pauses and the notes, how at times we could do it with others and at other times not, and when Julian started to push me away and I knew which way we were heading, I acted as if he'd already shoved me aside, as if we were already in the pause, and I got others to hold me till Julian was ready to take me back. We went to Aarhus together, and I took his hand down the street, but once again he pushed it away and snapped that he was fed up with my constant need for affirmation, and then he walked on and told me to stay three metres behind. At night we went to the local Pan Club, and Julian said we should find someone there to feed me some dick, but no one there was in on our games, and when I finally found a tipsy teenager with baby fat and bangs who didn't know any better, Julian had gotten tired and sat down at the bar so I took my new baby to the toilets alone, pulled his big soft butt cheeks apart and fucked him over the fixture while others knocked and asked if I had any idea what I was doing, but I ignored them because my skin was starved for affection, and my skin had made up a story where everything made perfect sense, where whatever I did was perfectly fine, and I tried to explain it to Julian afterwards, how it was really his skin I'd been starving for, how baby boy had only been comfort food, empty calories, but Julian's story had so little to do with mine that nothing I said made sense to him, and when we got to the station he told me it was over now, and this time there was no going back. Since it was our third time, I should've obeyed the principles of story-telling and accepted that over was over this time, but I begged and pleaded to still go through with our journey together, from Rome and all the way up through Europe, because even though I knew it would be torture, I also couldn't give up the thought that if I made him see how much I loved him, he'd be compelled to take me back. You've seen too many films, he used to say to me, just like his mother always said when his imagination took off, and maybe he was right, maybe my mind was too full of beautiful tragedies, maybe I just dreamt of waking up like River in *My Own Private Idaho*, alone and abandoned on an empty back road.

I slowly gather the courage to touch my asshole again. Explore it carefully with my index finger. I can feel a bulge down there, like a genital wart the size of a ladybug latched on to the opening down there, itching one moment and stinging the next. There's something bigger behind it too. It burns so much that tears start rolling every time I have to take a shit, but I still don't dare to feel around properly down there because even though it's been more than a week it just finally stopped bleeding, and I also don't dare to wipe myself with toilet paper yet, just rinse with the shower head over the bathtub. I'm afraid of how long my asshole will need to become itself again, afraid if my asshole will ever be itself again. I feel like a teenager who locked myself in my room, refusing to see anyone because I'm sitting here with this massive pimple on my forehead, scared I'll never be able to look another person in the eye again since the part of my body I usually connect to others with has suddenly become grotesque. Because, even though it's outside of my field of vision and I can only know what my index finger tells me, my asshole is, in lots of ways, just as important to my sense of self as my face, maybe because the affirmation I get when someone praises my asshole feels so unconditional and absolute compared to whatever is offered to my face. If I had to choose between life with a disfigured asshole and life with a disfigured face, I'm pretty sure I'd sacrifice my face, except I also know that with a disfigured face, it's unlikely how many would still want my asshole.

The first thing I notice is the box of paper tissues on the table between us. The white paper sticking up like a hand ready to be grasped, an expectation that I'm gonna cry, and it feels like I'm already doomed to fail. It's mostly because of my boyfriend that I sought out this therapist, to do something about the sex life that's been rather dead between us lately. I've told my boyfriend that it's extra hard right now that my asshole is literally good for nothing, but that's how it's been for pretty much a month now, and as he quite accurately pointed out, there's always a reason why it's extra hard right now. We start with me having to explain why I'm here, and I start with the stuff that's easier to talk about, my loneliness and my problems building social connections; I've always had a large network of people I see when circumstances allow, but apart from my boyfriend, I don't have any close friends who I regularly see. My second issue is that I use sex to compensate for my lack of social connections, that I try to elevate my sexual connections into also being social, and occasionally I even believe that it's working until I realise that none of them would ever invite me along when they're with their actual friends, and in the end, the connection always ends when we stop having sex. And finally there's the drugs; I tried quitting several times but always end up slipping right back in, not so much because of the drugs themselves, but because it's nearly impossible to find someone to hang out and have sex with without them sooner or later wanting us to do drugs together, and once I start liking someone, and maybe feel like they could even like me too, I simply don't know how to say no. I also mention the stuff about my boyfriend, but it's difficult for me to talk about after having talked about the sex I have with other people, since usually I explain to my boyfriend that my sexual drive just isn't that strong right now, but this doesn't fit with what I just said here, and even though it's important that I feel safe and feel like I can be honest with my therapist, I also don't want to come across as a giant asshole right from the beginning. The therapist wants to talk about the drug issue first since, usually when there's problems with addiction, this is where you start, but for this I'll have to be admitted to a rehab clinic. He says substance abuse is bad for the therapeutic process because therapy itself can be quite intense, and there's a risk that the addiction will only get worse. I try to pedal back and explain that it's really not a big deal with those drugs, that I wouldn't even call it an addiction, just a habit that sometimes gets out of hand, that it's been four weeks now since I last took something, which is actually true though it's probably just because my butt hole is still too messed up for me to get into something. I explain that it's not the drugs controlling me, but my need to connect, and that the drugs are just a symptom, a place I always end up, but not the reason I end up there, and even though it may not always be true I believe it enough to convince myself, and I'm not about to be admitted anywhere, under no circumstance am I gonna spend my summer in a rehab clinic, so if that's the direction he wants to go he'll have to go there without me (and besides, I'm not even sure I really want to quit drugs completely, at least not right now, or maybe it's just because I don't have the imagination to really see it happening). The therapist ponders and he says that if we're gonna continue together, he'll ask of me that I at least stay away from drugs as long as the therapy goes on, and I just nod eagerly and think that this will be an easy enough lie to keep up, especially if we continue meeting on Thursdays when I'll have plenty of time to recover from the weekend.

University played an important role in my story of the small-town boy conquering the capital. I went to daily double features, from Méliès and Murnau to Fassbinder and Fellini, I went to lectures on German Expressionism, French Impressionism, Feminist, Formalist, and Semiotic film theory, however, maybe because I still didn't have any idea where it was all gonna take me, it was harder for me to gather the motivation to pick up a book and read from any of the endless chapters that every week got added to our curriculum. It would be an exaggeration to say I was soaking up knowledge, but at least I sat down intently, let it flicker by, and reached out for the bits that seemed to make sense to me and my own understanding of myself and the world as I saw it from where I was seated. In particular, Narrative film theory inspired me with its distinction between plot and story, where plot refers to the images and sound presented and the order in which they're presented, while story is the connections and meaning the audience creates from what is presented to them. In other words, the film reduces its story to a plot after which the audience unfolds the plot and turns it back into a story. I started to view my life as a film I was constantly at work to arrange, since the similarities were striking between the process that condensed a complex story into a 90-minute montage of image and sound, and the daily work I had of editing my own chaos to make myself appear, both to myself and the world around me, as the romantic hero I, in the end, still believed I was. I still believed in the one and only, in monogamy, since I had nothing else to put in its place, but the paradox of the one and only is that no one can be monogamous without someone to be monogamous with, and if you're really gonna settle for just one, you shouldn't just take the first one that comes along, every option must be tried and tested, and in this way, the pursuit of the one and only can easily become a rather promiscuous affair, and if the world were to see me as a Romeo, some framing and slicing would be needed since a Romeo who finds another Rosaline every other day quickly loses credibility. One night at Cosy Bar for example, shortly after Julian had broken up with me for the second time, I found my first Alexander again, the one I only talked to for twenty minutes at the end of a party, walked to the night bus and kissed only once, and now we kissed again and went back to his room that was only big enough for a single mattress on the floor, and there he tried to fuck me in the harsh morning sun, and even though this didn't go very well, probably because of the coke still lingering like cookie crumbs around his nostrils, we still agreed to be boyfriends, and we probably were for a week and a half until we stopped responding to each other's messages, and when I met him out and about a few weeks later he suddenly had a girlfriend, or maybe he'd been with her the whole time; it didn't really matter though, what hurt me the most was that what used to be so special and sacred had now become so flat and pointless that one could simply stamp all over it and then walk on without even noticing. I started listening to Bright Eyes since he seemed to get the conundrum, and in *Perfect Sonnet* got closer than most to a solution when he sang that lovers should be tied together and thrown into the ocean in the worst of weathers and drown in their own innocence; that should teach them I thought, instead of running around, night after night, chasing each other in every conceivable constellation, like starry-eyed teenagers thinking they can have their cotton candy and eat it too, who just take and take and keep on wanting more more more since no one ever says no. My story barely held together in my own head, so for a wider audience to see the value of my love, see a love worth making movies about, I'd have to get out the scissors and kill me some darlings. For example, I'm not sure if Julian and I had actually broken up when I met Alexander again and agreed to be boyfriends, but that's how I now arranged the plot, since my own story, that our relationship was so solid our freedom no longer depended on if we were boyfriends or not, was way too complex to tell, and I knew it would come apart the moment Julian told his version. And all the while, I still had my own story where our love was strong enough that we could easily have sex with others, and I held onto this because it felt true in my own head, even though I knew it wasn't true by any common definition of what it means for something to be true. Storytelling is always an act of manipulation, selecting and arranging a plot with a beginning, a middle, and an end; just think of Romeo who, in the first act, cries his heart out over Rosaline but then has forgotten all about her by the time he dies in the end for his Juliet, or

John Travolta who, somewhere along the way, is mowed down on the toilet by Bruce Willis in *Pulp Fiction*, but because the plot isn't chronological, because it ends with the robbery in the diner that actually takes place earlier in the story, and because the plot in the end is more powerful than the story, it still feels like a happy ending when John Travolta and Samuel L. Jackson walk out the door together. There's no mess that can't be made up as a story, as long as the editing is done right, and this certainly applied to my life as well. Just like Bright Eyes, I still believed that lovers should be chained together and thrown into the fire with their songs and letters, left there to burn in their own arrogance, but if this was asking too much I could do with some trials and tribulations before finding someone I could love forever, even if, from the storyteller's perspective, this was less gratifying, because while tragedy is irreversible, a happy ending is always just a matter of editing, of plot structure, of ending at the right moment, and therefore happy endings will never be as true as pure tragedy. I started preparing for my first academic paper, which was on film analysis, at first with a plan to write about François Ozon's *Tropfen auf heiße Steine*, a claustrophobic drama based on a Fassbinder play about masochistic love between four people in a one-bedroom flat, but then I started reading about queer road movies instead, and after considering *My Own Private Idaho*, I decided to do a comparative analysis of Gregg Araki's New Queer Cinema masterpiece *The Living End* from 1992 and the Hollywood classic *The Wizard of Oz* from 1939. It was

Salman Rushdie's book about *The Wizard of Oz* that first sparked my interest in writing about this film, because while I'd long learnt to see Dorothy's escape from square and dull Kansas as a metaphor for the homosexual's flight to the city, it was interesting to read how an author living in exile from a death sentence related personally to the same story, and though I never meant to reduce the refugee experience to a mere metaphor for my own rootlessness, I still found it intriguing how the same story can speak to people of different backgrounds and how people of different backgrounds can find a connection by relating to the same story. *The Living End* and *The Wizard of Oz* are both driven by atypical film heroes, the former by a homosexual couple, the latter a female, and in both cases the journey begins with a killing committed by one of these heroes, but where *The Living End* presents itself as a product of a homosexual counterculture, a classic auteur film written, directed, and edited by Gregg Araki himself, *The Wizard of Oz* is ultimately the product of a self-operating Hollywood machine, and the iconic status the film now has among homosexual audiences can seem almost accidental. With four directors associated along the way and three writers who sliced and cut up Frank L. Baum's original story, *The Wizard of Oz* is pretty much as close as you get to the postmodernist dream of the authorless text. The ruby slippers that Dorothy clicks together to return to Kansas only appeared in the fourth version of the script and replaced the original silver shoes, probably to make better use of the film's Technicolour colours, while the arguably most iconic scene of the film, Dorothy's song about wishing herself away from her dull everyday life to a place over the rainbow, nearly got the chop when Louis B. Mayer (of Metro-Goldwyn-Mayer) thought the song was too gloomy and slowed down the film too much. Ironically, it's exactly these two elements that almost never made the final cut, which, in the end, define the film's meaning; on one hand, Dorothy's longing to leave the square and dull Kansas behind, and on the other, her longing to return home again, and while the studio believed conservative moral to be well preserved as long as homesickness won in the end, homosexuals around the world have embraced the film and created their own meaning beyond the plot by believing more in Dorothy's song than in the joy of getting back to Kansas, since they always knew this was Hollywood's ending and not Dorothy's. While Hollywood tries to discredit its heroine and drive home a conservative moral in *The Wizard of Oz*, *The Living End* literally starts by declaring itself an irresponsible film. The story is about the hustler Luke and the film critic Jon, both of whom are HIV-positive and flee together after Luke murders a police officer. The film is from back when unprotected sex was still a thing you died from, even in L.A., and death is also present everywhere in the film, with Jon who sits in his flat surrounded by skull decor while working on an essay about The Death of Cinema, with Luke who keeps juggling a pistol and always has a cigarette ready between his lips or behind his ear, and in the dialogue about other people's suicides and the freedom they themselves possess since now they have nothing left to lose. Where in the end *The Wizard of Oz* caves in to classic Hollywood ethos, *The Living End* sets out from a later tradition of road movies where the heroes can steal and kill without looking back and still have the audience with them along the way, but where lawlessness to Bonnie and Clyde and Thelma and Louise, much like Dorothy's adventure over the rainbow, is only on borrowed time till the film eventually sends them to their death or, in Dorothy's case, back home, it's striking how death refuses to take Jon and Luke in a film that's otherwise so saturated with symbols of the fatal end that inherently looms over both; Luke never lights his cigarette, Jon stops writing about the death of cinema and asks for a deadline extension, and even in the end when Luke ties Jon up and fucks him with a pistol in his own mouth, death refuses to do its part because when Luke, in the midst of orgasm, finally pulls the trigger, it only releases a soft click as a sign that the last bullet was already used. *The Living End* in this way refuses to clean up after itself but insists that Jon and Luke are still alive in the world after the film is over. The battle between longing for adventure and longing for home still comes through in *The Living End*, when Jon one moment savours his newfound freedom, and the next has had it with Luke and his recklessness, but when Luke, sarcastically and in a direct reference to *The Wizard of Oz*, asks Jon if he wants to go back to Kansas and live happy ever after, Jon has no response, and when Jon towards the end of the film calls his concerned best friend Darcy, who stands in as a symbolic Kansas, and says he's coming home, he says it in the dullest voice imaginable, without the slightest hint of joy. The film's final scene takes place on an empty beach, literally at the end of the road. After Luke's failed attempt at shooting himself, Jon manages to free himself from the knots, starts to walk away from Luke, and disappears out of the frame, but then returns and sits back down with him because, no matter how barren their Emerald City may be, the thought of going back to Kansas is still worse. What drives them is not an end they can ever reach; their longing takes them nowhere but away; all they know for sure is that the world is broken, or as Luke writes in big graffiti letters in the film's first shot, "FUCK THE WORLD." I never wrote a single word of this paper because the more I read, the more my thoughts kept branching in my head, like a road map that took me anywhere but Rome, and because it was all connected, it was hopeless to try and break it into sentences that only said one thing at a time, and in the end it made no sense to force so many thoughts down on paper just for one professor to read, so I dropped out of University and applied to journalism school instead, and by the way, it was their entrance exam I'd gone to Aarhus for on that day when Julian broke up with me.

For four hours they stand there together, trying to hitch that damn ride, but then Julian says that once he's seen five BMWs, he'll go back to Rome and take a train instead. At first Romeo is relieved that they won't have to draw straws to suck off truck drivers, but then Julian says he'll just find the fastest way home; he's had it with Romeo's bullshit. Romeo objects since the whole trip had been Julian's idea. Julian says this may well be, but it's been twenty years since then, and he doesn't see why they have to wallow in the past like that. Fortunately, it's when faced with opposition that Romeo performs his best, so at the station in Rome he pulls Julian into a printing shop and asks them to do a life-sized cardboard figure. Julian regards Romeo with both contempt and pity as they photograph his body and fix his red shoulders in Photoshop, and by the time the printer starts, he's long gone. The new Julian obviously can't walk on his own, so Romeo has to hold his hand as they go out looking for pizza. In the evening, they sit down at a piazza in Trastevere where Italian boys with piss-coloured hair and Green Day T-shirts play guitar and howl their songs at the moon. The police also stop by, sit for a while in their car with their eyes on the boys until they too have a song dedicated to them and drive off with warm apricot smiles. Romeo and Julian continue walking and look for a place to sleep. They find a makeshift cardboard bed in a park where Italian faggots flock around, fuck, and laugh in the bushes around them. The moon reflects on Julian's glossy surface, and Romeo is tempted to pull him over himself like a blanket, but he also knows it would be wrong to take liberties just because Julian is now a cardboard figure. Romeo thinks it's probably easier if the new Julian gets a new name too, and without thinking too much about it, he decides to call him Seahorse.

My therapist asks me what I've been thinking about since our last session, and I tell him I've thought about my shyness, how I always hold back and wait for others to take initiative, how I'm never one to start a conversation, never one to make the first call, how I always depend on others to take the lead, but that those who take the lead are usually the ones who reach out to whoever they feel like, and therefore their initiative never means as much as I'd like it to after all the time I waited. The therapist says that my piercings and tattoos maybe work as a filter, that they might be off-putting to others, and this may be why I only end up with superficial relations, and I'm thinking that this could be one of those red flags I need to react to, that I don't need a therapist who tells me everything will get better if I just tone myself down and try to be a bit more normal, but on the other hand, I did come here to be challenged, and I am aware that many people perceive me as tough, maybe even unapproachable, and of course this is something to question when my main issue is that it's hard for me to connect with people. I'm afraid my therapist sees red flags when he looks at me too, the red spots on my forehead, the bulging veins on my temples, the burn on my arm that I have no idea how I got and now have to hide under the sleeve of my sweater, even though I'm sweating like crazy in here, all because I obviously already broke the agreement to not do drugs while I'm in therapy, and I didn't just do drugs, I did them from Friday to Monday, and it was Tina who got me again, Tina who dragged me all over town on frayed knees and elbows. I still think about the boy who's suddenly there in the kitchen at the party that's been going on all weekend, the only one with his T-shirt still on, a black T-shirt with the logo of a rock festival, his hair bleached and orange, coming down his forehead and into his eyes, and I just want to be with him in an igloo tent at the rock festival instead of here in this kitchen full of drugged-up naked men, but I just walk on through the kitchen, back into the bedroom where I came from, lie down among the others and know I'll never dare to speak to the boy in the kitchen; I can't see what he would possibly want with me, so when he suddenly stands there in the bedroom, fresh out of the shower, in a washed-out jockstrap and with his hair tight in a rubber band on top of his head, and he says he loves my tattoos, lies down next to me and starts tracing them with his finger, it's by far the highlight of my weekend, and when he takes out his glass pipe and asks if I smoke, I hold onto the boy in the tent because this is still about him, not about Tina, even though, of course, I gladly accept when he asks if I smoke, and there's no words for how grateful I am when he allows me to shove my dick inside him, when he lets me go on even through it never gets hard, and when he whimpers as if he really believes this is not about my dick but about my skin that just wants to take in as much as it can of him while I look down at his beautiful white face, his skin like paper napkins dissolving in sweat and red spots, a body breaking down from the poison we just inhaled together, and though at first I dreamt of something different, this red light is what guides me

now, and though it may seem brutal, my need to see him
broken and destroyed is also a kind of love, or maybe just
a need to own him, which in many ways is just the same,
and though his number's written on a napkin somewhere,
I know the let-down it would be to see him clean or even
alive again, but of course, I don't mention any of this to
my therapist.

In the middle of the floor, there's a blond girl dancing. She's alone and too far gone on far too many substances. Two Italian guys dance in around her, getting very close. The one behind holds her while the one in front lifts up her dress and opens his jeans. They press her tightly between them while he fucks her, and she flops limply from side to side. When they're done, he buttons up his jeans, and they leave the girl just as far gone and alone as before. Two girls from the hostel saw it all from the balcony. Though Romeo is still puzzled by their story; it's just hard for him to understand how anyone can want to put their dick inside someone who doesn't actually want it there. They're in Florence now, and the girls from the hostel took Seahorse out to show him the club where it happened. The last thing Seahorse said before they left was that if they're ever gonna have a conversation again, Romeo first needs to get a brain. Pretty big words from a cardboard cut-out, but hurtful nonetheless. Romeo roams around all night with his filterless cigarettes, smoking away on one marble staircase after the other. He also finds a bar with a darkroom because when it comes to having other people's dicks inside him, he's still glad that there are places where he can just go and let it happen, and besides, he needs more now since he's also got a love to feed.

By the way, I started working with a film director on developing a film together. Our first idea was to make a TV series, but we changed it to a tragic love story, then a psychological thriller, and landed now on a romantic comedy where the lovers still get to have each other in the end. The only constant along the way has been our heroine, a stunningly beautiful transgender girl who we bent, folded, and trimmed over coffee and croissants to fit the three-act structure that all films, in the end, need to adhere to. In our latest version, she spontaneously left for her first trip to Berlin (as in, "let's ditch this party and grab a taxi to the airport" spontaneous), and now we just have to decide whether it's love or freedom she'll need to find there. I'd prefer a mix of both, but the director says that's not possible; we have to find the essence of the story. Maybe she first believes she needs one and then along the way discovers that it's actually the other, but a mix is never good on film. Writing a script is like solving an equation. A beginning, a middle, and an end; separations between them marked by two turning points. The second turning point points towards the ending, while the first sets out a course where it's clear there's still a lesson to be learnt. This means most tragedies are based on good intentions, whereas bad decisions mostly lead to happy endings. The director keeps reminding me that everything has to fit in this equation, otherwise it won't work on film (it's not like in novels where you can explain your way out of almost everything). Though the comparison to maths is probably too naive; there's something brutal, almost violent, in dragging narrative models down on someone, splitting life into phases and functions, how someone's want can never be the same as their need, how what they strive for is not what in the end fulfils them, never what can truly make them happy.

My asshole is finally on the road to recovery, even though it still itches like hell. I went to the doctor to have it looked at and he gave me a zinc ointment to treat it with, but it still won't stop itching, my stupid torn-up asshole, I just want to dig my nails in there and scratch back at it, stretch it out to feel something that leaves no room for anything else. I get out Seahorse and cover him with Crisco. I sit down on top of his head and carefully slide down his ribs that grow larger and wider the further down I go, and before long, I sit with my perineum against his heavy silicone balls, pressing down on them because there is nothing more to slide down over, and because I still don't have enough. It also hurts a little, but this just makes me hornier, and when I grab my dick I come in less than a minute, trembling like a beast, and I just want to move into my own asshole, build a nest in there and never come out, order everything online and never again look another person in the eye. It only bleeds a little when I stand up, and it quickly stops when I rinse with cold water. I decide that my asshole is ready to be used again, even though my index finger still feels a big scar on the inside and a strange skin flap that feels like a genital wart but isn't. I turn on my computer, just to see who's online, click on Vincent's profile, just so he can see I was looking, and it doesn't take long before I get a message from him. He tells me he's with the guy from last time, the one with all the STDs, and he asks if I want to come over too, and of course I do, I hover half an inch above the bus seat the whole way there, tear off my clothes and spread my legs for them, like a three-seater sofa for them, but they only manage to get one hand in each before it starts bleeding, not just drops of blood this time, but a stream flowing onto the towels, and though it stops again when I rinse long enough with cold water, it's clear enough that I still need more time to heal.

Third time my heart was broken for real was with Viktor, though, to be honest, I probably caused that damage myself. Viktor followed me loyally through a year of my life; from Aarhus back to Copenhagen where I landed an internship at the University Post, and night after night in the Latin Quarter where we dazed around in a haze of filter cigarettes and cheap vodka. Our first meeting was a blind date at a café in Aarhus. He didn't show for our first attempt, just messaged me and apologised for being nervous. The second time he told me to look for a small ugly boy in a raincoat, and though it was only the raincoat that fit the description, I still found his gaze as soon as I entered the café because, even though there was nothing ugly about him, something in that gaze clearly said that if someone in there had just described themself as ugly in a text message, it could only be him. He looked like a lost puppy, with eyes that begged to be loved and a body that shrunk and recoiled the moment you tried, and I felt the urge to take him home, hold him and caress him all night, but when I later pulled myself together and asked, he said he'd rather wait because, as he later explained, every time he went home with someone right away it meant he'd never see them again. I'd gladly see him all the times he needed before I was allowed, but when he finally invited me home to his bed, he ended up pushing me away and punching me in the chest while Beth Gibbons from Portishead sang about not being loved, not because of anything I'd said or done, but because my intent to love him and fuck him at the same time was just more than he could handle. He wasn't actually prudish about sex and beamed from ear to ear as he told me about the IKEA trip where he didn't want to tell them straight out he needed a bed with bars he could be tied onto, and he said that if I wanted to fuck him I should just ply him with more vodka since it wasn't like he didn't want me to, and in Copenhagen, I gave him what he'd asked for when we started our weekends with a bottle of the cheapest vodka from Netto which we mixed with the cheapest synthetic juice from Netto (Fun, it was called, and we decided orange was the least disgusting flavour), then headed to the Masken Bar where draft beer was still cheap, and there were ten shots for a hundred, then home on wobbling bikes to tumble down in bed where I fucked him like a mad dog, and we fell asleep with sweaty grins across our faces, amazed at how good we'd suddenly become at it together. But it also turned out that he'd been right, that mixing sex and feelings made everything more complicated, and the more we drank, the more those feelings took over, hung outside in all the wrong places, got tangled up, made us stop our bikes in the red light zone where we tugged and pulled till we thought we got them apart and could move on in our separate ways until we realised they were just stretched out like a long elastic rope between us, and he ended up giving in, let the feelings pull him back towards me, stumbled over a curb and scraped his knees against the pavement, and whether it was the feelings, the alcohol, or the scrape he whined about out there, I just stayed in bed and listened to the sounds from the bathroom and thought it was all just way way way way way way too much. We tried acting proper together, started taking boxing classes together (took turns punching each other in the guts while the trainer counted the seconds), and we went home to his and ate tuna steaks and spinach from Netto together, listened to Sonic Youth together, and agreed that when Kim Gordon and Thurston Moore sang over each other as they did in *Kotton Crown*, we felt almost bisexual since we couldn't decide which of their voices sounded more like sex. We tried acting dirty together, found a guy in a bar and went up to the sauna with him together, found a guy on the internet and went home to his place together, but this ended with us just sitting on his leather sofa, drinking Smirnoff with fancy sodas while we touched each other's thighs, because maybe we just didn't really want to, maybe we couldn't find the words for what we really wanted, maybe we got used to simply doing it, got used to needing way more vodka. I needed to get away, so I messaged Matteo from Italy, the one I used to think I could be boyfriends with, and he replied that he lived in Rome now, that I could borrow his flat while he went home to see his family, and so I left for Rome, just for a week, bought filterless cigarettes and smoked away on all the biggest marble stairs I could find, went to sauna after sauna and got fucked by one guy after another without it meaning more than another filterless cigarette on another marble step before moving on to the next, and when I got home, Viktor said he met our guy from the internet again, said he regretted it, and nothing happened between them, but he still thought I should know, and I thought he definitely shouldn't know about me and Rome, even though it'd probably have been good to talk about it instead of just sitting around together in my room not saying a word like we did now, him on the bed and me on the computer, like oversized goldfish in a way too tiny aquarium while the sun glared in at us, and I clicked from one window to another without finding a way out. It only got worse after I met Andreas in a cellar on Vesterbro where my friend Mads had called a meeting to start a group he called the Queer Liberation Front, and while all the punks sat around debating how much it sucked to be them, Andreas walked in with immaculate bangs and huge square glasses like a Lego person, prepared to take everything apart just for the hell of it. As the group started to crumble, we took each other's hands and ran off into the night together. He told me he was named after Andreas Baader, and we amped each other up with big words about revolution against everything that was hetero and normative, and he planted front kicks in every side mirror till we reached Vesterbrogade where he tried to rob a pack of cigarettes from 7-Eleven, and I felt like Jon in *The Living End* or like Thelma going over the edge with Louise, convinced that we could keep on going as long as we didn't look down. The Cinematheque showed a Godard retrospective, and Viktor and I had a couple's membership and saw more than thirty Godard films in two months, and I thought that for a director so obsessed with heterosexual relations, Godard, with all his deconstruction and performativity, was also remarkably queer, and it was no surprise that Gregg Araki and Bruce LaBruce made films that kept referring back to films like *La Chinoise* which first goes off like a table bomb of left-intellectual confetti until Anne Wiazemsky, Godard's new muse after his divorce from Anna Karina, one hour and seven minutes into the film, sits down on a train across from activist Francis Jeanson, and they stay like this for another fifteen minutes as the train rumbles along, and they talk about revolutionary theory and practice, and Anne Wiazemsky says she'll shut down universities by setting off bombs because when students and professors are killed, people are gonna stay away, and Francis Jeanson asks if she'll carry out these attacks alone, and Anne Wiazemsky says she'll carry out the attacks with two or three others, and Francis Jeanson says that this is not a lot, but Anne Wiazemsky replies that during the war in Algeria, when Djamila Bouhired blew up cafes, Francis Jeanson defended her even though the press was against her and all of France was against her, and Francis Jeanson says this is correct, but there was a difference too since Djamila had an entire population in Algeria behind her, men and women who already fought the same fight as Djamila, and Anne Wiazemsky says they fought for independence, and she wants her independence too, and Francis Jeanson asks how many people support her demands, if it's only two or three others, and Anne Wiazemsky says that many just haven't realised it yet, but she thinks on their behalf too, and Francis Jeanson asks if she believes she can start a revolution on other people's behalf, and Anne Wiazemsky says that if she wants to learn about revolutionary theory and practice, she'll have to take part in a revolution, and Francis Jeanson agrees with her but says she can only take part in a revolution, not invent one, and I sat there in the cinema and felt like they were speaking directly to me because, just like Anne Wiazemsky, I thought the world needed both rethinking and rebuilding, and, just like Francis Jeanson, I could see that it was impossible to create a revolution on behalf of people who had no interest in it. Andreas and I started a band together and rolled around on stage in thrifted clothes and fake blood and butchered teddy bears while shouting out slogans over homemade beats, patchworks of borrowed sound and stolen words. We stole words from cigarette packs when I screamed, *don't expose your children to sodomy*, and we stole from Philip Larkin's poetry when Andreas chanted, *they fuck you up, your mum and dad*, and we started going out together in fishnets and fake fur from the clothing bank on Istedgade, with plastic chains and cassettes around our necks and faces full of makeup, studs, and cigarette butts, and whatever else could be attached with spirit gum, and maybe it was because *Party Monster* just came out on DVD and became every club kid's favourite film, but either way, we just walked right past the line and got drinks in our hands and speed and pills for the rest of the night, then on to some after party at someone's flat, gallery, or hair salon, or we ended up on the beach in Malmö where our makeup burned into our skin and left traces far into the following week. Andreas and I also tried having sex together and agreed we weren't a fit, so I kept going back to Viktor, even though we broke up because I still couldn't find the words to say what I wanted, and because I still believed that cakes were baked and shared according to a centralised economy with one for each household, and it was up to oneself whether to keep the cake or to eat it, it was either one or the other, since no one had revealed to me yet that there are more radical ways to imagine community, that cakes can be shared freely among multiple households without anyone going hungry to bed, though I probably would have figured it out myself had I only dared to express my hunger with words, to say that I wanted a taste of everything and I didn't want to sit back with an empty plate because of it, but I was still too scared of words that expressed what I wanted, and apparently I still am, since I'm sitting here writing about cakes instead of love. I fell in love with a little punk visiting from San Francisco and discovered how grim love can get when you put it out there just for others to look at, and I wanted to find the words to apologise to Viktor, tell him how much I'd loved him and that I probably still did, but instead I went to London with Andreas to perform, did lots of speed and lots of ketamine, and eventually did acid and decided to move to Berlin, and in Berlin, words in Danish were pointless anyway, so I gave up on Viktor, and I gave up on journalism school, packed as much as I could fit in a station wagon, and as always, my stereo was the last thing I packed and the first thing I unpacked before opening a Budweiser from my new local corner shop, found Blueboy in my milk crate of LPs, put the record down on the turntable, and sank the needle into *So Catch Him.*

Though it's only been two days since I bled all over Vincent's sofa, and I've only slept two hours since then, my asshole still needs more attention than Seahorse and I can give it together, so I reach out to Angelito who I haven't seen since he tended to my wounds when they were still fresh. He welcomes me with his thong and cherub smile as usual, leads me to his stained sofa where I sit down naked and ready to embrace him as usual, to spread my legs as wide as they can go before it starts to bleed. Angelito asks about my asshole and I tell him that it's fine but also warn him of the scar and the skin flap and tell him not to worry about it. He asks if it was me who'd told him of the guy who got fisted and wouldn't stop no matter how hard it was bleeding, who refused to go to the hospital even though it kept bleeding afterwards, and because of this got infections in the wounds and in the intestines that spread into the bloodstream that gave him blood poisoning and killed him, and I say I've never heard this story before, but if it were me, I'd of course have gone to the emergency room long before it could get this bad. We take MDMA together, and we take GHB together, but still it hurts in a way that doesn't feel right when he fucks me, so when he asks if we should do another line I automatically say yes, even though he said he's trying to cut down, but this is fine because so am I, and I'm glad that Tina is never mentioned, though it doesn't take much scratching the surface to feel the longing still there. He fucks me, he comes, and we lie there gasping over the stains on the sofa, take more MDMA, more GHB, and he fucks me again, comes again, and the loop continues all afternoon till he says he promised some friends he'd meet them at a party, and I feel a pang in my heart knowing that the chemistry between us can never translate into anything beyond what we have together in his bedroom. Still I leave gratefully, walk towards the Hasenheide park where I hope someone will fuck me in the bushes even though it's cold and I have to zip up my bomber jacket, but then I get a message from the hot Brazilian punk who's messaged me several times already, who I always ignore because he always asks for dick pics, and dick pics are not something I carry around on my phone, probably because dick picks are not something I care much for myself, probably because I'd rather be adored for my butt hole than my dick, and of course he asks for dick pics again, but he's 300 metres away, and it's just started raining, so I lie and tell him my phone is almost out of battery and if he gives me the address of where he is I'll just stop by, and if the chemistry isn't there, I'll leave again, but there's plenty of chemistry there, with the hot Brazilian punk and with the bald guy with the transparent eyebrows he's with, with MDMA, with GHB, with K, with E, with the whole alphabet soup, and last but not least, my beloved, my cursed, my muse, my siren, a certain Miss Tina who I casually embrace, let blow smoke down my lungs before I voraciously throw myself between the two others who have long forgotten about dick pics and worship my butt hole just the way I like it, and my butt hole is just as worked up and sloppy as I want, like it's been soaking overnight and now just melts between their fingers, as if all skin flaps and scars have jellified into one giant aspic meat dish, and I can hardly believe how lucky I am that it never starts bleeding. When the bald guy with the transparent eyebrows finally asks me to leave, it's the morning after, but I'm still awake, and I'm still horny, so I take the U-Bahn to Nollendorf Platz where there're better chances of finding someone on Grindr who's awake and horny at this hour, but when I get off at Nollendorf Platz, my phone is out of battery for real, so I walk down Motzstraße hoping to catch someone with a lustful gaze and a flat around the corner, the good old gay way from before there was Grindr, but this of course doesn't work anymore, so I walk into the gay bookstore on Motzstraße and offer the silvery guy at work there a euro for charging my phone, and he takes the phone but doesn't want anything for it, and if it's because he'd rather give me the feeling I should buy something it's definitely working, and I consider John Rechy's *City of Night*, but instead find the latest from Brontez Purnell which is three euro more than on Amazon where I already have it on my wish list, but 16 euros to prolong my binge indefinitely is still a bargain, and on top, I get to feel super woke and intersectional feminist for choosing Brontez Purnell out of everyone to prolong my binge, though I also can't help thinking it's a shame how few people in Denmark will get it when I mention him, and I'm definitely gonna have to translate my book into English if I really want anyone to be impressed. I get a takeaway coffee from Romeo und Romeo on the corner and walk up and down

Motzstraße for half an hour, get my phone back and open Grindr where a two-metre-tall bald guy with huge pirate earrings says it's a pity he's not my type because he'd love to get brutally abused by me, and even though it's usually a turn-off when guys have already decided they're not my type, and even though I'm way more in the mood for being abused myself than having to do anything to anyone other than myself, it's Monday past noon already, and it's not a time to be picky, so I just reply that I'm totally in cunt mode myself, and if he wants me, this is how it's gonna be, which he accepts. I understand from him that we've spoken before, or maybe it's just in his mind or he thinks I'm someone else, but either way I get up on my toes and kiss him, suck up a massive line of speed from the kitchen counter and drop down on all fours, spread my legs as wide as they can go to show him what a huge cunt I can be, and he says that usually he's the biggest cunt, but he wants to use me as his cunt, and this is exactly what I want to hear since there's extra satisfaction in having a huge cunt use you as his cunt, the satisfaction of showing that you're an even bigger cunt, and he throws dildos at me, and I catch them and slide down over them while he moans *fuck yeah* and calls me a cunt and says that usually he's the biggest cunt, and he throws me down on the sofa and starts to work a hand into my hole, and when the last knuckle slips in, I say wait, pull out his hand and can hardly believe how lucky I am that it still isn't bleeding, and I give him the green light to go on. The next day, my legs are so stiff I can barely walk, but it's perfectly normal after I've spread them far too far apart for far too long. Still, I'm nervous the following day when I'm at the proctologist to check whether my asshole is healing like it's supposed to, because it's still so worked up and sloppy I'm scared he won't be able to tell what's what down there. I place my legs in the stirrups, and he opens me up and looks inside, and afterwards, in his office, he takes out a notepad full of perfect exemplary model assholes, draws a line across the top sheet and tells me it's a scar that's gotten infected, and he'll prescribe me Doxycycline and a new cream to treat it with, and then he draws a small loop at the end and says that this is the skin flap I'm feeling, and this he'll remove with laser surgery, but not today, and I can tell from his drawing that it probably wasn't too smart getting fisted again already, but I'm also relieved since I was afraid I could've gotten Chlamydia or Gonorrhoea again over the weekend and if this would delay the healing process, but if I do have Chlamydia or Gonorrhoea, Doxycycline also helps against those, and anyway, it's probably better I give my body a proper break.

The German boys sing, and the German boys talk. Some kids have plans to rule the world, some kids have plans to run away. These are words from a song on Romeo's Walkman, from a cassette he made when his first boyfriend dumped him. The words always make him long to be seventeen and a street hustler in Berlin. It's just a romantic dream of course, and it probably looks cooler in *Christiane F* than it is in real life. Romeo and Seahorse sit on different benches, staring off in different directions, and wait for the train to Paris. The lady at the ticket counter says the train left already. She says there'll be another in four hours. Romeo takes a cigarette from the pack but freezes halfway through the motion. Instead, he puts his hand and the cigarette on his stomach. He doesn't say a word to Seahorse about it, but the love he was forced to swallow just gave its first kick in there.

I'm back in Copenhagen to work on our film which apparently isn't a romantic comedy anyway because a romantic comedy is a very square box, and you can't fit whatever you like inside it just because it happens to be funny and romantic. We also changed the story again and now our lead is a model, in Berlin to shoot a perfume commercial, and while she's in Berlin, she falls in love with her driver who she first thinks is a giant loser but who we still force her to spend time with because conflict is what drives the story on film. We're ready now to apply for funding for writing the screenplay, and while the director writes to the Film Institute, I message Viktor and ask if he'd be up for meeting again, and the following afternoon we sit on his sofa together and talk as four hours fly by, and I can hardly believe it's been fifteen years since we last saw each other because it feels more like a few months, maybe a year at most, however long it usually takes for exes to stop being awkward around each other but definitely not fifteen years. The only time it gets awkward is when I mention my therapist and my loneliness, because even though I want to show that I got fifteen years older and fifteen years better at talking about things that are difficult, I'm still afraid of undermining my own worth as a person, especially with the loneliness part, afraid of coming across as desperate, as if I'm just sitting here as an exercise, as homework I've been assigned, and I can't have it appear like this (I reached out and saw that it was good, this is the story that needs to be told), so when he says I'm welcome to stay with him when I'm in

Copenhagen I'm feeling ecstatically happy because I want to build upon what I'm feeling right now, this instant closeness that feels so easy with him right now, and which I otherwise so rarely experience. As I leave Viktor's flat, I'm suddenly overcome by an urge to turn back time and pick up where we left it fifteen years ago, or maybe start again somewhere new that didn't exist back then, since maybe we just weren't ready to appreciate each other back then, maybe we both had things to sort out on our own first, and then again, I can't figure out if my prime desire now is to fuck him, hold him on a leash, or simply to be held by him, and maybe this is exactly the core of my issue, that I'm unable to find meaning in anything unless it fits inside this Romeo-shaped hole I have in my body, and maybe that's why I try to force everything that feels remotely important into that hole, wait for it to dry and come out again Romeo-shaped.

If home is where the heart is, the Danish rail company should name one of their IC3 trains after me. In 1990 when the model was rolled out, it felt like buying a ticket to the future. Everyone talked about how fast it went, and the advertising promised that your makeup could be done at 180 kilometres per hour. It was the year before my dad moved three hours away, the year before my sister and I started taking the train back and forth, and still today when I take the train from Berlin to Copenhagen, it's when I change in Hamburg and board the IC3 train that I get the feeling, more than anywhere else, that I've come home. Some dream of growing old in the country, others in a small house by the sea, but my dream is of a little red brick house under the railway bridge in Rendsburg, halfway between Hamburg and the Danish-German border. The two-and-a-half-kilometre-long high bridge was opened in 1913 and has stood there ever since, like a horizontal steel arch, sixty-eight metres above the Kiel Canal and the town of Rendsburg, and I can't imagine a more perfect place to grow old than there, to let my dreams be lulled to sleep between the railroad's rusty old elephant feet, while the trains just rumble on overhead.

As the Film Institute decides about our film, I linger on and try to nurture my relationship with Copenhagen. I usually say it's like an ex I once just had to get away from as quickly as possible and with all bridges burning; someone that now, with time, I have a more balanced relationship with, a wish to have back in my life again, not because we should get back together but because, in spite of all our differences, we still have a lot to build on. I have a few dates with old friends, a day planned with my siblings, a photo shoot for promoting a new book, and a shitload of time to fill in between. Mostly I just slouch around in a dull grey drizzle, buy second-hand books and read them in my maid's chamber on Vesterbro, spend half my time on Grindr but ignore every message, treat my asshole with different ointments and monitor how it heals. A guy texts me and says he's high as fuck, another sends pictures of himself with Tina in his hand, and he smiles as if it's all just love and happiness till death does its part. I reply with cold shoulders because even though I got plenty of time, I don't have time to break down and let my face grow back before getting photographed or before meeting with my siblings, and besides, the plan is that my asshole should heal properly before anyone's allowed to destroy it again, and all things considered, this should be easier to manage as long as I'm still in Copenhagen. I attend the launch as my friend Mads puts out his debut novel, *Sauna*. It's with a major publisher, and it's fantastic to see it happening because I read an early draft seven years ago, and I often say I would never have dared to believe I could write a whole novel myself if I hadn't seen him do it first, and suddenly I'm the one who's published three novels whereas his first is only coming out now, and while I'm genuinely happy for him, there's also a hint of bitterness that I can't imagine ever writing a book that's met with the kind of love his is getting right now, though I obviously also can't blame it on anyone else that I'm throwing everything into a book that's so damn difficult to love. I exchange hugs with people I haven't seen in years, say hello to others I'll never meet again, spot the fullest glass of wine at the bar, and suddenly everything is over and crumpled up somewhere behind me, and I walk alone back towards Vesterbro but end up in the sauna instead, with a towel around my waist, a rubber band around my angle, a key that chimes like a bell as I walk the dark corridors to nowhere. I return to the changing room and get the phone from my locker, open Grindr, and sneak a peek at the two guys tempting me with Tina, hoping they'll catch me lurking because even though I'm ready to put up resistance, I'm also ready to give in, I've become an expert at setting boundaries for myself which I can always cross later, I'll just dip my toes, only to the waist, and by then it doesn't even matter since I'm already wet, but there's no response now, so I slink back to Vesterbro with my nose buried in my phone, dreaming of getting lost in deep waters instead of just going back up to my maid's chamber and reading about the world ending while I treat the scars in my asshole.

They sit in the sauna cubicle, the three of them together. Romeo and Seahorse, and the young Frenchman they met in the changing room. The Frenchman asks if it's true they're all here to have sex. Romeo and Seahorse both nod. Romeo has hopes of a threesome, but Seahorse says that he and Romeo under no circumstances can touch each other. The Frenchman holds up a condom. He says that he'll hide it in his hand, and whoever picks the hand with the condom can have sex with him. Seahorse pulls the empty hand, he shrugs and says he'll wait for them in the steam room. Romeo would've rather come with him, since all he can think of while the Frenchman fucks him is what Seahorse is doing in the steam room and who he's doing it with. In the evening, the three of them go for a walk along the Seine together. They cross the bridge to Notre Dame, to the Island that lies there like a stranded ship in the black river. At the fore-end, people have jumped the fence to a small park. They dance drunkenly and twirl flaming ropes around in the dark, they pound on big drums and pass around crystal-clear liqueur. A guy with a radiant smile bids them welcome. He offers them a bottle but they say no, thank you, they just like to watch. The church behind them is still wrapped in scaffolding from the fire in 2019, but Romeo pretends like it hasn't happened yet. He doesn't get how Seahorse can hang his head like this when love is so thick in the air that you can eat it with a spoon.

A display screen told us to not leave our luggage on the platform or on the train. A bomb just went off on the London Underground, and a bag that wasn't anyone's could be life-threatening, and if anyone saw one, it was important to react. It was one of my last trips to Berlin before I moved there. I was there as a journalism intern, was there to interview the Palestinian artist Mona Hatoum. I also had a book in my bag that I really wanted to show her, though I didn't know if maybe it was just stupid. I started by asking about the Sonning Prize she'd just received, which was why the University Post had sent me to Berlin to speak with her. The prize is awarded by the University of Copenhagen for Outstanding Contributions to European Culture, and in this description alone, she found a great honour. "In England, art is often seen as something unnecessary, a drain on resources and taxpayers' money, so being recognised as someone who's contributed to European culture is a big deal for an artist. But also, for someone who's not originally European, it is a great honour to be considered capable of contributing to European culture. These two things are absolutely fantastic, that I'm the first visual artist and the first non-European." The prize committee's statement said that Mona Hatoum has found 'the most significant visual expression for the experience of New Europeans as living on that unstable ground between two cultures'. But her work contains more than that; "I also create my pieces for people who have just moved from the countryside to the city, for people who went through trauma, confusion, or despair." Many of her sculptures and installations revolve around the theme of home, but it's not home as somewhere safe or cosy since the doormat that welcomes you is made of sharp nails, the sofas are made of metal, and the child's bed has razor-sharp strings instead of a mattress, making it fatal to put a child to sleep there. The egg slicer and the grater look like themselves, but their blown-up sizes make them useless in the kitchen, and it quickly gets uncomfortable to try and imagine what the two-metre-tall grater is for. "It's obvious that I have issues with the idea of home as a sort of refuge from the world. I try and challenge this in my work by using ordinary everyday objects. Like the child's bed, on the surface it looks like a normal bed and draws you in with something nice and cosy, but then, as you get closer, you realise the object is not as you expected; it transforms and reveals something beyond the surface, something dangerous, something that evokes ideas of violence, pain, and perhaps even abuse." An installation that captures many of Mona Hatoum's ideas of home is *Homebound*, made up of pieces of furniture arranged as in a normal living room, but between them run a multitude of wires that electrify the furniture and light up a series of light bulbs; the lamps flicker, the current sings, and all of it is fenced off by a wire mesh. "I feel like there's a lot of different things at play here; just take the title, it could either be someone on their way home or someone bound to their home through house arrest. The fence also has a strange status, it can either protect you from entering the home or prevent those who live there from leaving, or just divide and create borders; you can see it as a metaphor for the homeland, for being exiled from it, or for the confinement of the housewife within the home." Mona Hatoum was born 1952 in Lebanon to Palestinian parents so home has always been a tricky concept for her. Her father worked for the British Embassy, which provided the family with British passports, and in 1975 she travelled to London for the first time. The journey had a huge impact on her life because while she was gone, the civil war broke out in Lebanon, and she would have to stay in London. It was a huge transformation, but despite the pain, it also opened up opportunities. "Suddenly, I was there alone in London. I was going to study art, and I was going to provide for myself. I had to fight hard and work evenings and weekends to make it, so it was a tough time when I felt like a stranger and alone, and it was a dark time with depression and people who didn't get what I was talking about because I was too loud or too expressive, but when I look back, it feels like it was all worth it because I actually managed to do what I wanted since I was a child, which was to become an artist." It's easy to read Mona Hatoum's own background into her work, but she doesn't like it when people try to reduce her art to a single message because often it becomes something completely different from what she'd intended. Take as an example the installation *Light Sentence*, a U-shaped wall of little metal cages stacked on top of each other like something out of a laboratory, but the cages are empty, and all the doors are open, and in the middle, a naked lightbulb is hoisted up and down, causing the grids to merge into a web of shadows. "Someone said it was about the prison-like conditions refugees live under, but for me, it was rather a reflection on coming to the West and seeing how people with low income were provided with this very basic housing outside the big cities, in France they actually call them *cages à lapins* which means rabbit cages." Joy and sorrow have always gone hand in hand for Mona Hatoum, both in her life and in her art, and a piece where this clearly shows is a wheelchair where the handles are replaced with serrated knives. "For me, it's full of contradictions. It has very small wheels so it is clear that a potential user wouldn't be able to turn them himself; he depends on someone else to push him, but how the handles turn into knives suggests that he hates this dependency, and it creates a very complex power relation." Also, *Light Sentence* with the rabbit cages and the shadows contains more than just a critical message. "Actually, it's a very beautiful and poetic installation, you have these harsh edges of the metal grids that become almost fluid on the wall because the light moves up and down all the time, and the floor feels like it's moving too. I'm trying to express a sense of restlessness and instability, and maybe this relates to my own displacement and the many transformations I experienced, but it can also be about questioning the stability of the ground you stand on. So of course there's a message, and the audience will always read their own stories into the artwork, that's how they explain it to themselves, but I also want to draw people's attention to the physicality and to the visual experience because it's important for me to explore the materials and their sensuality." She often creates her installations specifically for the places she exhibits, and the fear that inspiration will fail is always with her, but the fear also serves as an engine for her creativity, and like this she keeps recreating the pain and the uncertainty she experienced when she first arrived in London. "I reproduce the feeling of displacement and play with it constantly to see how I'll survive the next time and the time after that, so these kinds of challenges have become a part of my life." And this is where I couldn't hold back anymore. I had to show her what I brought, and I pulled Salman Rushdie's book on *The Wizard of Oz* from my bag. "It's funny," she said, "in the past when I tried to read something by Salman Rushdie, I couldn't handle it at all; in a way, it was too close to my own background and too emotional for me." But she was curious still, so I flipped to the final pages where Salman Rushdie summarises the meaning the film has to him: *the truth is that once we have left our childhood places and started out to make our own lives, armed only with what we have and are, we understand that the real secret of the ruby slippers is not that 'there's no place like home', but rather that there is no longer such a place as home: except, of course, for the homes we make, or the homes that are made for us, in Oz, which is anywhere and everywhere, except the place from which we began.* "It's nice when you read something and you completely identify with it. That's what makes literature so fantastic. By articulating different feelings or experiences you've had, it can make those experiences more concrete. Art can do something similar, but it does it in a language that's harder to grasp, it challenges rather than provides you with concrete answers." One of the writers Mona Hatoum has used to articulate her feelings and experiences is Edward Said who, like Salman Rushdie, has written about home as something that's been lost and that one can never return to. She forgot the exact words of Edward Said, but it doesn't matter since later, as we stood together in the printing shop where she took me so she could copy all of Salman Rushdie's book, she found her own: "The problem with home is that after you've left, it continues to change, but the image you have of it doesn't, so the idea you have of home becomes pure fiction."

They sit at Gare du Nord and wait for the train to Amsterdam. When the train arrives, Seahorse can't get up anymore. He's all broken down from the trip to the steam room, and he won't have it that Romeo tries to support him. But there's no time for being sentimental, so Romeo tucks Seahorse into a ball and dumps him in the nearest waste bin. He spots a pizza box that looks relatively clean, grabs it, and only just manages to hop on board before the train doors lock. Romeo rips the lid off the pizza box. He finds a magic marker in his bag and writes 'SEAHORSE' in big red letters. It's not the same of course, but a pizza box lid is still better than being completely alone.

It's a hot summer Sunday, and I'm back in Berlin, planning to take a walk in the park and dance to random people's boomboxes. Instead I get a message from Ivan who asks if I'm horny, and even though I'm not, I reply that I am because I'm ready to do almost anything to get there, and Ivan always has his bag full of drugs so no one needs to go without, and Ivan always has his bag full of needles so that no one needs to wait for the effect, and I already know before I reach out for the pipe that he'll suggest the needle, and I shrug and say sure, why not, as if it's a sudden impulse, a spontaneous idea, even though I know perfectly well that this is precisely why I'm here, because I too know perfectly well that the fastest way to a man's heart is through his veins. I already did a line of speed at home to get my bowels moving and also take a hit from the pipe before I go to the bathroom to clean. I bring along a butt plug to open my hole up extra wide, but perhaps I push it in too fast because when I wipe myself afterwards, there's bloodstains on the white towel, and it's dripping pink on the white glaze. The proctologist did say that the wound is healed, that there's only the skin flap left which he'll remove with local anaesthesia and laser surgery later this month, so I'm thinking it can't be that bad and rinse thoroughly with cold water till the bleeding stops. The right thing to do now would be to tell Ivan and the guy we're with that, unfortunately, it's not gonna work today anyway, but Seahorse is ready in my backpack, and Ivan already weighed out zero point one-two for me and dissolved it in a syringe with my name on, so in that sense, it's already written, and maybe we can still get through one round before it bleeds too much and the fun stops by itself. I sit on the kitchen stool in front of Ivan, and he takes my arm and disinfects where the veins show clearly beneath the skin. I've never slammed with a body this sober before, so my hopes for this meltdown are sky-high. He tightens the elastic band on my upper arm and makes me clench my fist, tautens my spine like a violin bow, lets it dance across a saw blade while my ears screech with sugar and neon. He lets the needle sink in, pulls back the plunger, and makes room for a tiny rose of blood to unfold in the clear plastic tube and bloom for a few seconds before it folds in on itself and disappears, along with the liquid, back into my arm. As long as the buckle holds the band tight around the veins, nothing happens, but in an instant (in a click, in a beat of my heart), madness takes over my entire body, a desire to be torn apart and put back together with my innards outwards, to be stretched ten metres long and kneaded into a lump no bigger than a pair of socks, moulded into an exact copy of Seahorse with a Seahorse-shaped hole in my heart. The others ask if I'm okay, and I gasp and nod, tell them I need to be stretched out immediately, take Seahorse under my arm and go to the bedroom, crawl onto the black rubber sheet and place him in the middle like a milestone, a silicone obelisk I slide down onto with the greatest ease, and when I get up again, there's not a drop of blood in sight, and suddenly, seven or eight hours have passed that I only remember in fragments, Ivan is gone, and I'm alone with the guy we're with, and I say that I should probably be going as well, but as I sit at the S-Bahn station I'm not quite ready to go home, and besides, I have speed and ecstasy in my bag which I brought to pretend like I hadn't already chosen Tina, so I dip my key twice in the speed and check on my phone how to get to Tiergarten as fast as I can. The last picnic guests are still packing up as I arrive, and the ping-pong table is occupied by shouting teenagers, but I have all the time in the world so I take off my shirt and sit down against a tree while Joanna Newsom sings in my ears that she can see I'm wearing my staying hat. I swallow a quarter of ecstasy and feel like taking off the rest of my clothes right away, but I have enough time to wait for the darkness, I have the whole night ahead of me and a strong belief that all the dick I need is gonna come to me without me having to chase it. A man approaches me in shorts and sneakers, he kneels down in front of me, grabs hold of my feet and tries to make me kick him in the chest, and I let him for a while because it seems so wonderfully absurd here beneath the tree with the bark against my back and Joanna Newsom in my ears, but then the hollow of his eyes becomes heavier than I can handle, so I smile gently and shake my head, say that if he's looking to be dominated he's kneeling in front of the wrong tree, and I repeat this five or six times before he gives up, but it doesn't bother me since I have all the time in the world to repeat it as many times as he needs. I take off the rest of my clothes, put them in my backpack, and wander through the night, feel certain that we're all here for the same reason, all shiny tracksuits, all sweaty bodies, all pants down around the ankles, we're here to meet in this gentle darkness, against the trunks, beneath the canopies, to open our bodies and let each other in, to draw lines and make a web that disappears as soon as the sun comes up. I make my way to the ping-pong table in the middle of the lawn, swallow another quarter of ecstasy, climb up and lay face-down with my chest against the cold concrete and my ass towards the sky, spread my legs and push my ass towards the stars. Shadows come out of the darkness, slowly circle the table, disappear and return, they stroke my back, grab hold of my butt cheeks, glide fingers into my hole as they caress me with words and sounds, and I take them all in my mouth and between my legs, lay out my gratitude so there's enough for everyone, find Seahorse in my backpack and place him as a monument of victory on the concrete surface, and I place myself on top like an angel to be worshipped from all sides, complete and connected, hung from the stars with threads running down my legs, and I notice a boy bent over the table on the other side of the net while another boy fucks him, and I feel like I recognise the boy getting fucked, he looks like the boy with the red spots, the one from the party with the T-shirt from the rock festival where we should sleep in a tent together, and I crawl over the net and whisper his name in the darkness, and he says yes but is too busy getting fucked to look up, I don't want to interrupt them, I just sit there, overwhelmed with affection for this boy while the other one pulls his hair and he howls into the cold concrete. Later, I find him on a bench, and we go for a walk together, talk about how beautiful it is in the park at night (the darkness, the silence, the feeling of magic right in the middle of the city), and when the sky slowly starts to brighten and he wants to find his bike, we hug and kiss goodbye and auf wiedersehen, and I'm thinking how this night is so bestowed with magic I don't even need drugs to feel high, even though I'm perfectly aware that whenever someone says they don't need drugs to feel high they're usually already on drugs when they say it.

In a way, I'm lying just by writing in the present tense. Not right now, but when I pretend to report from the eye of my own ruin, because just to send a message to my boyfriend and assure him everything is fine, I need to sit for at least five minutes and gaze into the screen while crystals float around like melted wax in there, just to make sure it's even a real sentence I'm sending out, and when I finally come home, there's several days when my body and my words are so heavy it seems impossible they'll ever be of use to me again. And yet, when I do write in the present tense as soon as I have the strength, it's because I need to see myself in the midst of the meltdown again. I know people who film their friends when they collapse from an overdose, because without the images they just repress or forget it; it's a way to show them afterwards that this is not a joke, and it's probably what I'm trying to do for myself here.

When someone I know offers me a cigarette, I usually just tell them no thanks, but when they ask if I quit, I tell them it's been more than fourteen years, and usually this is longer than I've even known them. My standard narrative is that I quit smoking because I was in hospital for two weeks with pneumonia. It was my first Berlin autumn, but it dragged on through an entire winter where the capacity of my right lung was still not back to normal, it hurt when I tried to take a deep breath, as if my lung was pressing down on an open wound at the bottom of my chest, and my doctor told me he couldn't promise I would ever fully recover, and when people hear this, they never question why I haven't touched a cigarette since. It's rare that anyone asks why I was in hospital for two weeks because of pneumonia, but when they do, I usually just shrug and tell them it was an exceptionally bad case of pneumonia, because this is how I remember it myself: the coughing that escalated in a single day from zero to a hundred, my chest that coiled up tighter and tighter as if someone had put chains around it, my flatmate who kept asking if it wasn't about time we went to the E.R., but I'd be fine I said, until around midnight when even the slightest movement cut through my chest as if someone had put barbed wire around it, and I nodded through another cough attack that, yes, maybe it's time he order that taxi. When I don't explain how my pneumonia could escalate this fast and how it could last this long, it's because I remember it mostly as a thing between myself and my lungs; all the tests and diagnoses that were done were all about getting me my lungs back, and when the scrubs asked if they could do an HIV test, I just nodded through my coughs; of course they could do that, they could do whatever they thought was necessary to find out what was wrong and get me my lungs back, and when they told me the morning after that the HIV test had come back positive and they would transfer me to a special department at the Auguste Viktoria hospital, I mostly just felt relief, since the more they knew, the more they'd be able to do to help me. When I don't explain how my pneumonia could escalate this fast and how it could last this long, it's because it just doesn't work to tell a story of how I quit smoking and then have to explain that pneumonia struck exactly in those weeks after I contracted HIV when it's perfectly normal for the immune system to take a dive, at least not without my story suddenly changing from being the story of how I quit smoking to being the story of how I contracted HIV. I gratefully accepted the single room I was offered (probably so I wouldn't cough barbed wire down other people's lungs), they poked a needle into my hand and fixed it there with tape so they could fill me with antibiotics, and even though I didn't immediately get my lungs back like before, the coughing did wear off, and I felt relief that there were people with a plan for my body, and all I had to do was to lie there and get better without anyone expecting more of me. Lisa Germano sang from my laptop about black and blue bruises, and I looked up and saw this guy who stood and gawked out in the corridor as if he'd just stalled out there. He held himself up by his IV stand, both hands around it in a knot, his hospital-cloaked body trailing after it in a feeble arch (from his gaze that hung like the blackest cloud on the horizon, down to his feet that just stood there, lost in a pair of woollen slippers with no idea where to go from here). I remember his skin being covered in spots, though they could easily have been added to my memory for the image to better fit the story of our shared condition, but either way, he definitely looked like someone at the end of his rope, and it seemed somehow wrong to me that he would stand out there like this, since I knew several people, my flatmate included, who were positive, and even though I'd sometimes still behave as if we were talking about death when talking about it, I also knew that this wasn't the case anymore, that you no longer withered and disappeared (not in Europe at least, not like back in the eighties), and even though this one out in the corridor probably wasn't even older than me, it still felt like looking into the eyes of a ghost, like staring into decades of collective suffering, as if he'd been sent there to remind me of the history of this virus I'd now have to carry for the both of us, and at the same time it was clear to me that the darkness in his gaze was as vacant as the sky, that everything I saw in there only existed in my own mind, and even though I would, without hesitation, have shared his suffering between us if I could, I also knew that this would never be possible, that to me, it would always be a history of those who went before me. The scrubs wanted to know if I had anyone I could talk to, and I didn't know what to tell them, because even though I knew several who were positive too, it wasn't immediately clear what we should talk to each other about. Later on I said to my doctor (tentative, hopeful) that by now, having HIV probably wasn't much more of a risk than smoking a pack of cigarettes a day, and he told me there was no doubt about that, that more likely, it was the other way around, that a pack of cigarettes a day was quite certainly a much bigger risk than having HIV, and I wondered how long they had known this was the case, since it hadn't been that long since I read articles about men who fucked like rabbits without ever using condoms and also knew that it was probably just a question of time before they were infected (and maybe even looked forward to no longer worrying about if it had already happened), and in the articles this was described as the most insane behaviour anyone could ever imagine, as something no normal person would ever be able to comprehend, and I got angry that they described it like this at a time when it was probably already known that the risk wasn't bigger than smoking a pack of cigarettes a day, because even though smoking a pack of cigarettes a day is also stupid, no one would ever write like this about smokers, and I got angry because I thought maybe this is why so many of us have had a hard time balancing risks and desires, because our desires had been ruled out in advance, labelled insane, something no normal person would ever be able to comprehend. Many people asked me back then if I knew how I got it, and I always told them I didn't know since this was the easiest explanation; with no idea where I got it from, there was nothing to regret, no one to blame, but although it was the easiest explanation because it best described how I felt at the time, it wasn't actually true, since the scrubs had also drawn blood for a Western blot test, and it confirmed what the sudden dive of my immune system had already suggested; that I'd been infected within the last few weeks, and in that time, there'd only been one guy who fucked me without a condom. He'd found me at a party far into the morning when my mucous membranes were already so frayed from speed and filterless cigarettes they were just waiting for any excuse to bleed. His mohawk was soft like plush, his skin moist and ready to smear all over mine, and I followed him home to his flat in Kreuzberg where he cracked open two beers, which we took a sip from each and left on the coffee table, then continued into his bedroom where the day was slowly breaking outside, nothing it made sense to call dawn, just a raw concrete autumn grey which it felt completely surreal to be this vibrantly alive in, this brave and defenceless in, to disappear under the weight of a foreign body into torn fitted sheets (into washed out blue terry cloth), and I gasped like I was trying to disappear completely, and he held me down like this, forced his cock inside me, and even though he didn't immediately stop when I told him to stop and put on a condom, I didn't give it much thought either, not until I was told at the hospital that I'd been infected within the last few weeks, and though it seemed like I should be angry about what happened, this seemed completely alien to me because even though I didn't let it happen on purpose, there'd been so many times before when it could just as well have happened, and it could just as well be because I hesitated too long before saying stop, as because he didn't stop immediately when I told him to, and I also met him several times after that, and no longer told him to stop when he started fucking me without a condom, and once I felt how liberating it was to let myself be fucked unconditionally, to lean fully into it, it just seemed absurd to think that I should regret anything.

I hear my name, and just as dawn dissolves another orgy in Tiergarten, he's right there between the ping-pong tables by the toilets, glowing all paper-thin and cotton-white, the boy with the red spots in a jockstrap and a T-shirt, and we hug and kiss before he nods towards a blond guy who looks like he's trying to escape through his own pupils, and he says we need to be discreet because the blond guy can easily get jealous, and since I've only taken ecstasy, I feel like I can totally be discreet, even though it might not look like it as I stand there on the lawn, naked and covered in dirt, sweat, and scratches. The boy with the red spots says they're looking for a friend who has his pipe, and he asks if I want to come along, and he pulls me behind the toilets where we find the friend with the pipe, and the pipe is full of sunshine that unfolds an extra forest in my lungs, and I don't even notice when the boy with the red spots disappears with the blond one again, just follow the friend (the pipe) into the toilet where he doesn't care that my dick is too limp to get inside him, he just wants to plant more sunshine and see the trees unfold in my chest, and I just want to lie down on the tiles and take root, but he says we should do it outside in the grass instead, and we find the others on a bench, along with a man who's probably around sixty, but either he's the most beautiful sixty-year-old in the forest, or everyone is just beautiful here in the forest, and he brought his own pipe which he connects to my lips so the forest can continue to grow in me, and he passes it on to the boy with the red spots, and he asks him about the red spots, and when the boy with the red spots replies that he got them from Tina, I can't contain my desire for all this beauty right here in front of me, dressed in its own downfall, like a long-stemmed rose slowly dying in a vase on my desk as I sit and write about love, and I think of a novel by Dennis Cooper where they talk about an eighteen-year-old rent-boy and say he's still cute but give him a year and a half before Tina has ruined him, and I think about how those words make me sad and horny at the same time, and I think about a friend who, twenty years ago, told me about a trip to Berlin where the clubs were full of guys fucking without condoms, and how back then it still sounded like mass suicide, like a crazy rush from collectively fucking the world, and I think of dead leaves and burnt-out stars, want to collect it all in a marmalade jar, let it turn to dust and become life, but then the boy with the red spots leaves with the blond guy who's still trying to escape through his own pupils, and I go with the sixty-year-old back to his hotel and continue to suck on his pipe instead.

There's something incredibly beautiful about allowing oneself to be fucked without questioning who's doing it, to reach a point where one no longer confuses physical beauty with human qualities, to let go of the pride that otherwise makes us see attractive people as more deserving of our skin, and experience instead how every person's skin is worthy of our touch, that no one deserves to be let in more than others, even though this state just lasts for a moment until I look up at the sweaty face above my shoulder, the rotting teeth and the reddened nose, and the beauty I briefly saw in our connection dwindles between my fingers, turns cold and clammy, and I just have to get away as quickly as I can.

My doctor calls and says I have Gonorrhoea, and I'll need to come by for a shot of antibiotics. He also says my liver counts have gone up, along with something he calls muscle counts, I have no idea what that is but he says it could be caused by excessive exercise or caused by drugs, especially Crystal which is just a fancy name for Tina. I make up a story about how I just got back to the gym after a longer break, but what I'm thinking is, there it is, damn Hepatitis; just as I almost forgot about being scared, I'm convinced again that I have it, but at the same time relieved because it's only when I test positive that I at least for a while can let go of being scared completely. It's probably my wounded asshole that made me not think about my liver, forget that still getting fucked with an inflamed and constantly bleeding sore up your ass is obviously gonna increase the risk of a disease that only spreads through the blood. My doctor asks if I've been doing drugs as well, and I admit to the speed and the ecstasy but deny everything when he asks directly about Tina. He wants to do a new blood test when I'm there for my injection, and then he mentions what I'm constantly thinking about, that my elevated liver counts could also be because of Hepatitis C. Fortunately, the treatment is not as harsh anymore as back when I had to take pills twice a day for nine months and inject myself with inter- feron in the stomach once a week, and I didn't know if I got depressed because it was a common side effect, or if I got depressed because I expected to get depressed after my doctor told me it was a common side effect, but even though the treatment is better now you still have to wait half a year to get the pills, half a year where nobody wants to put anything inside me unless I stay quiet about what I carry around in my body.

In seventeen years, a giant meteor is gonna hit Earth. It'll destroy an entire continent, completely alter our climate, and wipe out most of the life we know today. It's on the news on Dutch TV, and Max is translating it for Romeo and Seahorse. Romeo knows Max from last summer in Copenhagen when he met him in a bar and sucked his dick in the bathroom, and Max gave Romeo his number and said Romeo was always welcome if he needed a place to stay in Amsterdam. Romeo and Seahorse have talked about going out tonight, but Seahorse is still stoned from the space cake they shared yesterday. It hardly comes as a surprise since Seahorse is just a thin slice of cardboard now, but either way, he'd rather stay home and watch a film with Max and his boyfriend. Max tells Romeo that if he wants to go out, he better leave early, ideally be at the club half an hour before it opens, since there's always more people in the line than there's room for inside. At the club, Romeo meets a guy named Ivar. He's wearing a Sisters of Mercy t-shirt that says 'fuck me and marry me young' on both sides, and he asks if Romeo wants to go to the bathroom and do some ketamine. Romeo has never done drugs before, except for hash, but he's open to whatever Ivar has to offer. They dance to the electroclash cover of *Sunglasses at Night*. Romeo imagines a musty mattress in a candle-lit loft where Ivar can feed him drugs and fuck him as the world ends, but as soon as the song is over, Ivar swaps him for a German. When Romeo gets back to the flat, Seahorse tells him he had sex with Max and his boyfriend while Romeo was out. The words hit Romeo like a punch that continues straight through his body. It feels a bit like ketamine, but in a super bad way. Romeo floats toward the balcony and feels his feet let go of the ground. He quickly lights a cigarette, inhales as much as he can and fills his body with smoke, just to make sure he's still there.

I've had a strange itch in my throat and have been coughing for almost a week. Feeling tired and too heavy to get up. My first thought is whether I picked up another round of Gonorrhoea or Chlamydia, so I stop by my doctor to get tested even though it's only been two weeks. Just to be sure, I ask about my liver counts because they haven't called me after the last tests, and this usually means everything is fine, and it's also what he says when I ask, that when they don't call, it's because everything is fine. He still checks, just to be sure, and tells me that my liver counts were significantly lower the second time. I ask if this means everything is fine, but it doesn't he says; they were lower but not fine, so I better come back in another two weeks to get tested. And once again I'm convinced that I have Hepatitis C, but I think that so often, I'm trying not to overthink it.

Saturday night I sit with a beer in my hand between a bunch of people I don't know, around a coffee table at a party I've gone to in order to meet people without having to be at a party, at least not what I usually think of as a party, since we're still sitting here with all our clothes on and we've only done one line of speed so far. A guy I don't know texts me and tells me to come to his party which is only 300 metres away, and he sends me pictures, with and without clothes, front and back, and he's hot in a way that usually doesn't interest me, but he keeps saying how he wants me, and I always find it hard to say no when hot guys insist they want me, regardless of how little they otherwise interest me. They're about to do a slam now at his party, and he asks if I want to join. He wants me, and he wants to slam with me, and fuck all night together with the rest of his party, and he asks me if it doesn't sound hot. Sure it does, I tell him, but the thing is that whenever I slam, I'm just no good for fucking, I just become this giant gaping fist hole that can't get enough, and it doesn't seem like that's what he's after, but he tells me this sounds mega fucking hot and promises that my hole will be wrecked to pieces if I just come on over. It's been a while since I had my hole wrecked, and I do feel like having my hole wrecked, and this is why I don't just tell him that I really don't want to, even though I decided that I'm done with Tina, and I'll do what I can to stick to this decision, at least for the moment. Instead I keep going on about how out of my mind I get when I slam, how I forget everything apart from being a hole that needs to be wrecked, and he tells me over and over again that it sounds fucking hot, that I should just come right away, but I'm really just playing with the thought and know very well that it's not gonna happen, at least not tonight, because I want to be done with Tina, at least for now. I take the night bus home instead and hope the entire way that my boyfriend's gonna wake up when I crawl into bed with him, hope he'll reach out under the covers, grab hold of my arm and nestle it around him, but when I finally arrive home the bed we sleep in together is empty and he has moved to the guest room (where he sometimes goes when he doesn't know when I'll be home, when he doesn't know if I'll be home at all). I lie down in our double bed alone, still with too much interference to find peace within my body, I just lie there and hope he'll wake up to go to the bathroom, wait for the sound of his sleepy sighs in the hallway, the faint creaking beneath his footsteps, the flow that always hits the side of the bowl and never directly into the water, and all the other extensions of his body asleep behind that wall, try my best to connect somehow before I eventually fade into a sleep of my own.

Romeo sits on the balcony, gasping. It's too hot out there to smoke, but he can't be bothered to move. Seahorse says that for him, the journey ends here. Romeo doesn't feel the same, but it doesn't matter, since the story of Romeo and Seahorse was always the story of Romeo and how he was dumped. Seahorse says he's still too stoned to go anywhere, and he also appears to be in rather bad shape, though this is probably because Max and his boyfriend didn't consider when they had sex, how fragile he is. Obviously, Seahorse can't just hop on the train by himself the way Julian did, so Romeo has to take him to the post office, buy stamps, and send him home in a letter. First he thinks he'll have to pay extra because Seahorse doesn't fit the standard envelopes, but then he borrows some scissors and trims him till he fits in an A4. And with that, Seahorse disappears from the story, perhaps rather unresolved, but there's really not much left except the idea of Seahorse, and this Romeo won't let go of so easily.

The guy from the slam party texts me again on Tuesday. Either his party just died, or they're preparing for another round. He tells me how he still wants to slam with me, how he still wants to wreck my hole, and it's still hard to say no considering how relatively hot and super motivated he is, but even though we easily agree that my hole should be wrecked and that he should be the one to do it, I still avoid anything related to Tina, ignore it until he cuts away everything else and asks directly about Tina; don't I think she's hot, isn't slamming just too fucking hot, isn't it just the greatest. I reply that if I'm being honest, I feel the same way, but if I'm being honest, I also feel how much she destroys inside me, and no matter how good it feels with her, I pretty much always end up regretting it afterwards. I don't expect to hear more after this, but instead, he tells me he also regrets it. He tells me he regrets it every fucking time. He's a junkie, he tells me, no point in denying, a total fucking junkie. He tells me that drugs are the worst shit there ever was, that he can't live with them or without them, that they ruined his life completely, turned everything into shit, shit, fucking shit, all of it. I don't know how to respond other than by saying I'm sorry to hear this. Meanwhile, I'm thinking about everyone who slammed me until now, the ones who disinfected my veins like a nurse would, and poked me with sterile needles, those who unleashed the devil inside me and told me it was so fucking hot, those who shared their pipes in bedrooms, in parks, and on dance floors, oozing with tenderness, warmth, and pornography; I think about how many of them also woke Tuesday and regretted everything, how many of them still walk around and feel like junkies, how many of them believe that drugs have ruined their lives and turned everything into shit (shit, fucking shit) and still go on and share them as if they were gifts of love.

I've come to the conclusion that everyone is fucked up, it's just only the most fucked who're forced to do something about it.

It's finally time for the proctologist to remove that damn skin flap from my butt hole. The assistant, who doesn't look a day over twenty, makes me take off my pants and sit down on the examination table. He asks if I have an iodine allergy and raises the table so I can't reach the floor, then leaves me there in my underwear for fifteen minutes till the doctor comes in. The doctor gets me to place my legs in the stirrups, then pull down my underwear, just enough to expose my ass. He says there'll be a tiny pinch and then pushes the needle into the soft folds around my hole. It burns, but only for a short moment before the anaesthesia starts working. The laser starts buzzing, and the assistant turns on a machine that sounds like a vacuum cleaner, holds a plastic tube near my butt, while the doctor does something to my hole I can't feel because of the anaesthesia, and yells something I can't hear because of the noise, and the assistant says he's asking if it hurts, and I answer no, and then the doctor continues while a foul stench of burnt flesh and pork rinds fills the room. It's all over in a couple of minutes, then my ass is stuffed with iodine and gauze, the assistant lowers the table again, and the doctor gives me a new ointment to treat it with and says I should give it a good week to heal. After that, at least my asshole should look normal on the outside; then there's just the scar on the inside, but he told me it's healed, and once my asshole is properly worked over, no one's gonna feel the difference anyway, even though last time I went to Tiergarten, I did suddenly notice there was blood all over my balls, but of course, this could have come from anywhere.

I dream that I wake up one morning and my name is William. I dream that William goes to a party and walks around completely naked, wearing only socks and shoes since it's the kind of party where you can easily walk around like that, and lots of people do, though most just dance in outfits of rubber, leather, or almost nothing, but still more than William since it wasn't his intention to be at this party, he just passed by and felt like dancing, and since he didn't have any rubber or leather in his bag, he just left everything at the door. It's the first time in a while that William is at a party without drugs, and he's looking forward to coming home in the morning, satisfied and exhausted, instead of chasing around all day for more, but then this is when V enters the dream (in real life V also has a real name that could've been Viktor even though it's not, but it's shortened here to V because it's my dream, and you can't hold other people accountable for things they do in your dreams). V comes dancing towards William, his body wrapped in strips of black tape and his crotch covered by a jockstrap, he can't be much older than twenty, William thinks, and yet he smiles as if he's been there from the start and knows exactly how it's gonna end. V yells his name into William's ear while their bodies have a taste of each other and a woman sings over the speakers about how love can take them higher. They settle on a ledge overlooking the party, and V asks what William does when he isn't at a party, and William ends up saying he's a writer, and V asks what kind of stuff he writes, but William doesn't really want to talk about his first book where drugs probably took over a bit too much, and which is otherwise a pretty conventional story about love, with a beginning, a middle, and an end, which he has since realised is rather trivial compared to how complex love can be in real life, and now he wants to write like a recording device, just report what he experiences, but there's no way he can sit here and say all this out loud without feeling too high above everyone else. V tells him he's a shoe designer, and then they start making out. V has his hands on William's crotch, one hand stroking William's cock (and William thinks it's wonderful to be free from the drugs that always made him horny but also unable to do anything apart from taking and wanting more), while the other hand pushes one, then two, then three fingers inside William's asshole, and William can feel how they long to continue all the way up there, and he can see it in V's eyes as well, and he decides that he'll ask for V's number before he leaves, and the thought crosses his mind that maybe this is not a dream they're in, but the beginning of the kind of fairytale life can be if one can manage to be present without expecting too much. The week after, while he's at a concert, William gets a message from V, and though years ago he swapped dick pics with the singer on stage and it's sort of implied they'll be going back to the hotel together, only twenty minutes pass before William rings the bell at V's place, throws himself into bed with him and stays there for about an hour, and when he leaves, he's no longer the same; later he'll be telling V that it felt like he'd been led by the hand through parts of his own body he didn't know existed, and William will apologise and say he knows it sounds silly, not so much because he thinks it actually sounds silly, but because he's afraid V will think he means it as a metaphor, and William doesn't like metaphors, so V has to understand that when he writes about how he feels, it's something very concrete inside himself he's describing. Two days later, they meet again and continue punching into each other's openings; V can go all day, and so can William, as long as he does it with V, and they start doing it several times a week together, and William is ecstatic about how far over the edge his body can go without leaving the physical plane. When William tells V that he's becoming addicted to him, he's very much aware that it may be a bit of a metaphor, but he thinks it's just a small innocent one, even though he knows all too well that metaphors are never innocent, and before long, William starts feeling sick and nauseous when it's too long between his visits, I want to see you, Boy Harsher sings in the song that V always plays on repeat, and William starts listening to it in his headphones when it hurts too much to be away from V. They go to a party together, and again it's the kind of party where one can walk around naked and do it all over the place, and William is only wearing socks and shoes while V has black latex gloves that go up to the elbow and a black rubber jockstrap, and V brought speed and ecstasy and offers some to William, and William can't say no, but it's not so much a pill as it's a corner of the night he gets in his mouth, that he clenches his back teeth around, and they throw themselves out on the floor together, and they hide in dark corners together, and V keeps on finding new paths through William, and they go home to V's bed together and collapse in each other's sweat together, and William clings onto V while his back teeth rub against each other, and as V falls asleep, William thinks that even though he could easily get addicted to all this rubbing, it's also just an exception. But then V starts getting out the pills at home as well, and even though William first says no to one, he also thinks a quarter is innocent enough, just a tiny little corner, but V says pills don't have corners, and suddenly he's taken a whole one, and Boy Harsher sings that you'll hurt me either way, but it's okay because it's still about V and not the drugs, at least for William, and William knows all about when the drugs take over and become what everything's about, like that time he ended up married to a woman, and he ended up killing her by accident; they'd been awake for days and had gotten lost in a game that might once have been sex but wasn't anymore (though it's hard to say, since with the kind of drugs they were always on, there was nothing that was really sex, just like there was nothing that really wasn't sex), and William still hasn't figured out how the judge could let him go, and he'll probably never get an answer because he doesn't remember much from that time, and everyone else seems quite content that in the end, apparently nothing was anyone's fault. Then one Monday evening at V's, there are more drugs on the table than William has seen since they met. V gulps down a whole ecstasy pill with a tall glass of gin. He looks like he didn't sleep all weekend, and when William says no thanks, V snorts a line of speed twice as thick as the straw it's going up. V says his job is killing him; a deadly virus just broke out in the country where the company he designs shoes for is based, and two co-workers who just returned from there are now in quarantine. V swallows another pill and empties another glass of gin. V's eyes are hollow, and William wishes he could want something more than just to wait for V to finally get wasted enough to join him on the bed. When V is finally ready, he squirts a curry-coloured mix of water and shit all over the bed and William's thighs, and William cleans up as best he can and suggests that maybe they should rather get some sleep, but V won't stop now, and William opens himself to him as best he can, but V falls asleep with his arm inside him, it's a special talent V has that he can sleep no matter what he's on, and William just lies down, clutching him in his arms while love blooms madly at all this vulnerability V is showing as he lies there unconscious. Next morning, V turns on the computer and says he wants to invite other people over, and he writes to everyone and tells them to bring drugs if they want to come over, and then he leans back on the bed and waits; William recognises the first one from back when everything was still about the drugs, and he's not surprised when the glass pipe comes out, and V brings it to his lips and inhales while all tension disappears from his face (as if he, with sigh of relief, lay down to die), and Boy Harsher sings it's just a matter of time, a matter of your time, and William doesn't say no either, but all he feels in his lungs is a longing to get closer to V, around him and inside him at the same time, but V is too busy entertaining, and William just goes along with it, lies down beneath him like a pillow, hopes for attention, hopes that V will collapse over him and let him bear some of his weight, but instead, V keeps slipping further into himself along with a parade of shifting characters until they briefly wake up together on the bed with a joint between them, and Lana Del Rey sings that you don't have to be stronger than you really are when you're lying in my arms, and it's enough to make William cry, how accurately she describes them lying there with the joint between them, even though it's clearly not a coincidence, just like it's not a coincidence when you're high on a dance floor and a woman sings over the speakers about how love can take you higher, since the music was made for standing on a dance floor and insisting that it's love that makes you high, not the other way around, and, in the same way, Lana Del Rey's songs are written for lying in each other's arms with a joint between you, or for lying alone with a joint and wishing you had someone to hold. From here on, the dream gets more and more obscure; every time William reaches out for V, he's gone, and V excuses himself with fear of the virus that's constantly drawing closer, that's suddenly everywhere around them as they sit on the bed, and V shakes the needles, shakes the crystals, and gets ready to blow William's heart out, and William closes his eyes and for a moment, he's Nikolaj, who sits and writes that V pokes the needle into William's arm, like the astronaut who plants the flag on the moon, like the victory column where the roads meet in Tiergarten. And William wakes up with a scream since William wants nothing to do with Nikolaj's tired old metaphors, and in reality, it's V who sits there with the needle in his arm, gasping and sighing for all the fiction his body can bear, but then I wake up myself and realise it's all just a story I'm writing, and if I want to make it out of here alive, I'll have to leave V behind and head for the exit, as quickly as possible and without looking back.

Romeo is taking notes for a story he calls *Dogs of Love*.
Though it sounds like a metaphor, the dogs he imagines
are absolutely concrete. He imagines that they're invisible,
but this is not what's most important; the special thing
about the dogs of love is that they neither mate nor
reproduce like other mammals but are brought into the
world by love itself. Every time love ignites between two
people, a new puppy is born. And as long as love burns,
the dog is strong and healthy, its fur shiny as silk, and its
teeth hard as marble. But as soon as love is extinguished,
the dog loses its source of life, and it must feed on the love
of others to survive. It's not the force of love that sustains
it anymore but the rush of destruction, and it's not
uncommon to see it leave love fatally wounded and simply
watch it bleed to death. But even the bloodiest rush won't
fully satisfy the dog; the only thing that can save it now is
if the love that brought it into the world is ignited again.
Romeo's story should begin with himself and his freshly
broken heart. He weeps about how nobody wants his love
and is convinced that if the world could only see how great
it is, no one would ever turn it down again. The second part
should be about the dog howling over Romeo's heartbreak
while at the same time trying to feed on the love of others.
But when the dog understands just how great Romeo's
love still is, it swears by the moon never to harm another
love again, and, therefore, bringing Romeo and Seahorse
back together becomes its only chance to survive. Romeo
imagines a real Lassie story, one that all parents will want
to read to their children. He imagines comics, movies,

and toys that children will want for Christmas, and when every child knows how great his love is, when bringing Romeo and Seahorse back together is everyone's favourite schoolyard game, it just seems impossible that Seahorse won't come back to him.

Vincent texts me again and asks if I'm up for something. It's the first time I hear from him since I bled all over his and that other guy's hands, and I can't deny that the urge is still somewhere inside me, though it's slumped down in a darkness I didn't know I had until now that it stirs down there. I lie on the sofa, stare at the phone, at the question, at the passing of time. You can't tell by looking how destroyed I am, and once Tina has pulled me up, I won't be able to feel it myself either. I look at my thumb as it moves across the letters and types that I'm down, and I look at my thumb as it hits the arrow that sends the message. He sends back pictures of his butt hole in full bloom, and I send pictures of my own from before we lost it on the floor together. My thumb agrees on when to meet, and I can tell from the clock and the passing of time that I'll need to get started, need to get in gear, but still, I just keep lying there. My urge still flops around, somewhere down there, but I have zero desire to reach down and get it. My thumb types that I'm sorry, that otherwise I'd be down, but that there's just too much I need to get done this week. I look at my thumb deleting the message, and I look at my thumb typing it again. It's a game of chance (a roulette that spins, red, black, red, black, loves me, loves me not) until my thumb finally lands on the arrow, the message is sent, and a sigh echoes down in the darkness.

When I wake up from the dream, I find myself in the midst of the global pandemic that shan't be named because of how sick and tired of it we all are, and I actually swore never to write about it because I was fearing a flood of trivial novels all about relationships that crumble in nice flats while the crisis outside runs like a parallel arc, a symbol of inner dissolution, but even though parts of this book were written decades ago, it was only as I found myself in the midst of the pandemic that I pulled myself together and tried to make a book out of those parts, and therefore it seems like too much of a lie to now ignore it completely. So there we were, in the midst of a global pandemic that the radio said was the biggest crisis in Europe since World War II, but there weren't any air raids, sandbags in the streets, or tanks rolling in from anywhere; just people taking walks, every day was like Sunday, and you wouldn't know from the sight of it that it was a criminal offence to get close to someone or to sit down on a bench and enjoy the sun. Perhaps this is how everything came to seem so pointless, because we just sat there together, my boyfriend and I, alone and isolated in our nice flat together, and fell apart together, while no one was able to tell. And that's when my loneliness became so concrete, when we were told to stay in our bubbles and only see the people closest to us, and some of us discovered that we didn't have a bubble, that we weren't among anyone's closest, that we had no one but ourselves and the fiction we sat working on, and so we filled our stories with names and plural pronouns to feel part of something until words stopped making sense, and there was no difference anymore between a poem and a recipe for chocolate cake. Apart from our vacant sex life, this was also why I started therapy, to figure out why I wasn't among anyone's closest, but then my therapist forgot to plan more sessions, and when I wrote and asked him why, he'd just left on a month-long vacation, and it felt like even my therapist couldn't be bothered to see me, and besides, it was stupid of me to have lied about the drugs because after I started lying about the drugs, it felt like we had an unwritten agreement that it was okay for me to lie, and it became too easy to just avoid whatever I didn't like talking about, like why my desire for my boyfriend and my desire to fuck couldn't be in the same room together, and instead, our conversations just kept going back to my past, back to my father, and I have even less desire to write about him than I have about the pandemic. It's been several years since I last spoke to my father, and I actually thought I'd already put a period there and moved on, and the world doesn't need more books about confronting paternal issues either, or maybe it does, but books about paternal issues should probably be written by authors who're actually interested in confronting them, not just in ending them with a period and moving on. But when I lie to my boyfriend (when I lie about Tina), it's hard not to think that it's connected to my father, to how my three siblings and I have all given up on keeping contact with him, to my sister's children coming home from school and asking, 'what's a grandfather?', to how close we were to losing him after he hit the bottom at the end of his second divorce. I was still living in Copenhagen when I got the call from my father's ex-wife, the one who, 15 years before, had lent me her jewellery and introduced me to Leonard Cohen, and she told me that my father had had a heart attack, he'd been having dinner with her and their children at her new place when it happened; out of nowhere, he got up and said he'd left something in the oven at home, and when he came back, he started speaking gibberish and couldn't hold his fork anymore, and it's hard not to think that it might as well have happened in the car on the way back there. The next day, I visited him at the hospital in the other end of the country, or rather, I visited the body that used to be his, because there was nothing left of his language, and there was no recognition in his eyes; the only thing he reacted to was the nurse's cleavage, which he grabbed for as if it contained the only way out of his misery, and I couldn't make out if what we saw was pure infantile innocence, if he was hungry and just wanted to feed, or if he'd digressed into a wild and untamed animal, a horny pig in its absolute purest form. It's shocking to look at one's father and realise that he's not there inside the body you recognise, but at the same time, this is also why grief and tears seemed so far away, because it was so clear to me that the shape in front of me was not my father. After a couple of days, he did return to his body, and we returned to life where we'd left off and never talked about what happened, not until years later when he started disappearing from us again. No one knows why my siblings and I aren't welcome in his house anymore, the house where my middle siblings grew up and saw him hit the bottom after his second divorce, the house where he now lives with his third wife and our youngest sibling, who we stopped counting since we haven't seen them in so many years, the house where the last traces of us were removed after he asked my sister if she wanted the pictures he'd taken of us when we were small, since otherwise he'd throw them away, and even though I think it's a shame those pictures no longer exist, I can also very much understand why she didn't take them. I was the last one still allowed in the house, probably because I lived so far away and mostly just came home for Christmas, but then he started making excuses for why they no longer had room for me in their 370 square metre home, and after me and my siblings went with him on an hour-long walk, where we all tried really hard to be a family, he suddenly disappeared into his phone and came up with an excuse for why he couldn't stay for dinner as he'd promised, and even though I was angry, it was also a relief when he left since we no longer had to try hard, we could talk freely about what the fuck was going on, whether it was wife number three who refused to share him, or if it was him using us as an alibi to see a mistress; there were theories that he'd already long ago fucked all the wives on their street, and maybe this is why they've now put the house up for sale, or at least my sister saw a sign in the front yard one time last year when she drove by, so who knows, maybe it's already sold, we have no idea since none of us have been past there since, not even my sister who lives only ten minutes away by car. The last time I spoke with my father was in 2019 at my brother's wedding, where I sat next to him for five hours without exchanging more than three sentences, and once again I had the feeling that it was just a body that looked like my father with nothing I recognised inside; my boyfriend was seated on my other side, and since no one else was very good at remembering to speak English, this was my excuse to constantly turn away from my father, and on my father's other side sat my younger brother, and it was his celebration so of course everyone demanded his attention, and like that, my father ended up sitting completely alone between us, he just sat there smiling to himself as if everything was just the way it should be, but as soon as dessert was cleared away he vanished without saying goodbye; they'd prepared for all of us to spend the night there, but suddenly his bag and his car were gone, and I said to my sister afterwards that at least he must've realised I was over him by now, but she thought this was underestimating his capacity for self-deception, and we laughed about it, though it also fed an anxiety that had started to take root in me, the fear that something was passed down from him, that whatever broke between us is also about me calling him by his name instead of 'dad' already when I was ten, and I'm not writing this to place blame, I'm simply considering whether whatever has pushed us apart has less to do with our differences and more to do with the things we have in common, how both of us would rather drown inside ourselves than reach out and ask for help, how both of us seem to carry the same existential loneliness, the same pathological desire to, no matter the cost, portray life as a story we're always the master of. I usually say that my biggest problem when it comes to drugs is my ability to keep it under control and continue without it getting out of hand, that I can stop when the party's over and ride out the comedown as it comes, but that because of this, I can also go on without ever really hitting the bottom; I can decide to put drugs behind me and still do coke or meph with a date, I can take just one shot of G and tell myself that it's just an exception, go on till I'm suddenly gone all weekend and realise that apparently I didn't want to quit drugs anyway, at least not completely, at least not right now. I've tried several times to put the drugs behind me but I can't confidently claim that I truly want to succeed, since there are still too many people I want to explore first, people who won't open up without them, and in the end I'm probably one of them, since opening myself up to others is a sport I've trained for for years now, opening my body and inviting others into my flesh, making my muscles relax and my openings bloom, and it's under the influence that I've mastered this training, so it's under the influence that I know how everything works. I know when to take the first line of speed, how to suppress hunger and not need to eat again after breakfast, how to speed up my bowel movement and be clean by the time I need to be, and I know when the pumpkin seeds from my muesli come out half-digested, that I'm ready, and then I just need a quarter of a pill to lift me up because I haven't eaten all day. I also know that when I try to start without drugs, it's only a matter of time before I'm offered, it's only a matter of time before I say yes, and then I end up in the bathroom and spend most of my high with my ass over the bathtub, flushing out half-digested pumpkin seeds along with everything else I'd been eating all day, and every time I just wish I'd started earlier and taken the first line in the afternoon so I'd already be clean. I've tried several times to put the drugs behind me, but every time it works, I fall asleep and dream again of another V, another someone I want to explore, and then the cycle starts all over again, and the pandemic isn't the end of anything, just a new beginning before I run away and crash down on another filthy sofa, and in the end, it has very little to do with sex, at least very little to do with the need for skin and closeness I still feel with my boyfriend, so when I tell him that my sex drive isn't strong at the moment, that the skin and the closeness are still what's more important, it's not completely a lie but it's not completely true either, not as long as I only say it to cover up the power drugs still have over me, and this is why I so rarely mention my boyfriend when I write, because in the end it's not about my relationship with him when I write, but about my relationship with drugs, my relationship with all the others (the urge to run away together and move together into a house that's already on fire), it's about the times he had to go home alone because my body had decided on other bodies to explore, about the times I stayed awake all night and lied about sleeping at friends' places, the times I lay awake with guys long dissolved in the passing of time, the scratches and the wounds I came home with and lied about, the time I lied about having taken an extra strong ecstasy and been afraid to go anywhere, when really I just wanted to stay and get fisted one more time, the time I was drugged and raped for hours and lied about it afterwards because I thought my boyfriend would say I'd asked for it, because deep down I probably thought myself that I'd asked for it. I'm ashamed of my lies because I know from my father that the hardest thing to forgive is the lie itself, but when I lie to my boyfriend (when I lie about Tina), when I lie down naked in the sun without sunscreen because my father's skin cancer has nothing to do with me, it's hard not to think that at least his capacity for self-deception has been passed down to me. If he told us why we're no longer welcome in his house I'm sure I would accept it, since it's the lies and the secrets that have made him a stranger, and still I expect my boyfriend to accept the Nikolaj I choose to present as the true Nikolaj, simply because it's the Nikolaj I choose to present, because in the end, no one knows Nikolaj as well as I do, and in the end, it doesn't feel like a lie but an honest attempt at giving him a Nikolaj I still believe I can be. When I lie to my boyfriend (when I lie about Tina), I'm really mostly lying to myself, because I can't live with how real my meltdown will be if he knows about it too. I come home with a body of lies and try to only show him my love, and at the same time I want to turn this body inside out and expose all the lies since I don't have room for both stories inside me anymore, but still I'm afraid to own up to the lies, not because I'm afraid of his reaction, or that he won't forgive me, but because afterwards I'll have no way to hide in the lies anymore, and at the same time I know perfectly well that this is exactly why I need to do this, why I need to finish this book no matter how much it scares me. Sometimes I'm scared of losing respect for my boyfriend because he keeps falling for a liar, but then I remind myself how grateful I am that his trust is bigger than I deserve, his trust in the love that, even though I'm not sure exactly what the word means, I never doubted is true, and that I know I need if I'm not gonna end up in a relationship with someone like myself, a relationship where the drugs get to spread out and take over everything till I'm finally just in a relationship with Tina who slowly consumes me until, in the end, only she remains. Tina is the only drug that truly scares me, since the longing she roots in me punctures any claim I have of having any sort of control. I used to have a principle with Tina that we only got together when I found her among strangers, and though it may not sound like the smartest it still somehow made sense, because as long as I only met her out and about, she had no way of finding her way back to me, but then she started imposing herself on the people I knew, I had to end it with a lover because I knew that whenever I came by, Tina had already invited herself, and she would take up more and more space in the bedroom, so much that when the thing between us ended, I wasn't sure anymore if it was him or Tina I missed the most. The first time I slammed was with a guy who was a trained nurse, since I thought he'd have to have a grip on needle stuff, the second time was with two guys who had a huge flat full of expensive furniture, since I thought they'd have to have a grip on life in general, and since then I've gotten bolder and braver, allowed myself to be poked by guys with faces like Frankenstein's monster, with trembling hands and sweat dripping down their waxy foreheads, but of course, these were all exceptions, and if anyone asks, I've done it three times in total, tops, definitely not more than a handful, and I almost believe it myself when I say it, pretend like nothing is wrong while my hypocrisy oozes like bile, how I constantly distance myself from Tina and those in her circles, until I find myself at the bottom of another Friday night or a Sunday morning, and I'll do anything for anyone who can take me to her, and usually I don't have to do much since most of them just long for someone to take their poison with, someone to indulge in delusion with, and not say out loud what we see in each other, and it's not about big dicks, trimmed bodies, or beautiful faces; on the contrary, the closer we get to the ultimate meltdown, the more we look prepared to die together, to burn up in white roaring flames together, not for each other, but alone and entirely for our dear beloved Tina. I can't help thinking about Torsten who I met when we starred as extras in the same film, and again a few months later when we ended up together one Monday morning at a bar that never closes, and he fucked me in the toilets and on the sofas and got others to do the same while he prepared for our next shot of G, and we took turns collapsing, took care of each other, and shared a taxi back to Neukölln where I saw him a few months later in the park, disappearing into the bushes with pupils bigger than buttons, and he turned harder and whiter like porcelain in every photo I saw of him online, until he turned up again at the flat of some random guy who was just supposed to fuck me, but it all became about Torsten who wouldn't leave before he'd turned over every piece of trash in the place that looked like a never-ending after-hour had just died there, because Torsten was convinced that remains of Tina were still hiding out there, and no matter how often he told us he'd leave so we could get on with the fucking, he kept sitting there, turning over the same pieces of trash as if he thought we couldn't see him, and that was three weeks before New Year's Eve, which I celebrated with my boyfriend and some of his friends on the streets of Kreuzberg where we were joined by a homeless middle-aged homo who started sobbing at us about how he didn't have any friends, how he didn't have a boyfriend, and though I'd rather just have brushed him off on someone else, my boyfriend insisted that we take him to the nearest shelter, and when we rang the bell, there was no staff there, just a bunch of homeless people at the door, and one of the homeless people there was Torsten who gave me a silent nod, and I gave him one back without my boyfriend or his friends noticing, and then I didn't see him for a while, not until last week in the park when I was just there to enjoy the sun and he suddenly came stomping through with rigid limbs and arms flailing around like a psychotic toy, and I waved at him discreetly, and he waved back with his whole arm and stomped on into the bushes, and this repeated a couple of times until I sat up, and he came over and sat down next to me, and I asked how he was doing, and he roared some unintelligible sounds and looked like he was just as freaked out by how fucked up it sounded, that it wasn't words coming out of his mouth like he'd expected, and when he stood up and walked away, I just thought he probably had an unusually long weekend, but when I was back in the park today to buy weed and he came stomping through in the exact same way, with a faded ALDI bag under his arm, it dawned on me that the park is probably the closest thing he has to a home right now. And then I can't help thinking of the Ukrainian skinhead and the video he uploaded on Facebook last week, just him staring wide-eyed into the webcam, saying that his neighbours have been trying to kick him out of his flat, that they've been stealing his mail and filming him through the windows, and he just found out that a lot of the guys he hooked up with had been sent by the neighbours to spy on him, that they've filmed him doing drugs and getting fisted and put it on the internet, which is how he lost his job now, it's all arranged by his parents, the German state, and the medical industry that want to force him back to Ukraine where they've done medical experiments on him since he was a child, trying to re-code his brain, and if they catch him they will continue this until it kills him, and then I can't help thinking of my 23-year-old former neighbour who, after I fucked him, told me about a time in London when he, after three days with Tina in some strange guy's flat, had a psychotic episode and jumped from the third-floor window and almost died from internal injuries, and I can't help thinking of the guy who raped me for hours while I was unconscious, and of his ground-floor flat that I kept cycling past to remind myself it had actually happened, until one day I cycled by and his balcony was full of flowers, cards, and candles in red plastic, and I stopped and had no idea what to feel because, just as I was convinced that it was Tina who made him rape me for hours while I was unconscious, I was also convinced that it was Tina who'd finished him off, and it didn't make it easier with all the cards from all the people who couldn't believe that he was really gone, and it was hard for me to comprehend that the guy they all missed so much was the same guy who raped me for hours while I was unconscious, and it didn't make it any easier that, even after he raped me for hours while I was unconscious, I still messaged him and asked him to fist me again because at that time I couldn't find anyone else who was up for it, and I gave him permission to continue no matter how hard it was bleeding because that's how he wanted it, and it was only because he suddenly went offline and disappeared that I didn't go ahead and let him do it again. I still insist that I'm not an addict, that I'm only using, not abusing, but even though I haven't taken anything for a month now, it's still not the end of anything, just another beginning before I meet another V to swap wounds with, another brother to share blood with, and even though I convinced myself now that I don't have Hepatitis until the doctor says I have Hepatitis, the question now is only if it's the next blood test that gets me, or the next, or the one after that, and just as love takes different shapes in different hearts, addiction too has countless forms, from the body that can't bear to be in the world without its drug, to the one that simply lost the ability to say no, that slobbers out of control every time another Romeo presents himself, and then it's just like Abba sings in *Mamma Mia*, here we go again, how can I resist you.

My liver counts are back to normal. Or at least they were on Friday when they did the last blood test. I was afraid they'd do another test today because I fucked up with Tina again last Saturday, and I did it again on Monday. When they told me the results today, I mostly just felt tired. I'd expected a final confirmation that I'm just not able to take care of myself, an excuse to give up completely, pass on responsibility, or at least take it on properly, not just crumple it up in an ALDI bag and think I can pull it out whenever I need it. I was so sure that I'd be positive this time that I already planned to use it as a framework for my story, to let it serve as an awakening and turn it into a happy ending. I even thought about still ending the story like this, regardless, but I just don't think my body can handle more fiction right now.

The train glides out of Amsterdam, and in thirteen hours Romeo will be back where he started. Though he dragged it out for another week, he only got to touch Max's dick once through his cycling shorts as they waited for the elevator. Romeo sits alone on the train now with a Romeo-shaped hole in his body, not sure if it's a clone or a counterpart he's missing. He read that when matter meets antimatter, both disappear and become nothing, and maybe that's the solution. When two identical sine waves lay on top of each other, the volume doubles, but if one shifts so they oscillate out of phase, the sound disappears completely. In this way, twosomeness and nothingness are less than a second apart. On his Walkman plays the song about the German boys who sing, the German boys who talk, and about the boyfriend who looks like James Dean, and Romeo imagines the German boys look a lot like the ones in *Christiane F,* with leather jackets, skin and bones, and synthesizers in their ears. Romeo would like to just stay on the train in Hanover and continue to Berlin instead of changing as he's supposed to. In Berlin he'll give birth to the love that's right now kicking inside his stomach, he'll provide for them both by sharing his body with strangers; everything he does will be for love alone. When he thinks of Berlin, it feels like running over an edge and just keeping on running, and even though the metaphor might be a bit tired by now, I'll let it stand because it's really how he feels, and besides, it gets an extra layer here since his entire longing for Berlin itself can be said to be somewhat of a tired metaphor.

The point of this book wasn't to write about disease and pandemics, it wasn't to write about fucked up families, nor about sex, drugs, or addiction, but as I wrote in the beginning, to write about the love I still like to believe will conquer everything. It's late September now, and even though every day feels like the last day of summer, we still haven't seen the end. This has kept me off the drugs for almost two months now, the same way writing does when it feels like I'm on to something. I type these words at the table I share with my boyfriend, in the flat I share with my boyfriend, while other people's lives pass by outside the open window. Some stop and offer me weed, a stolen mobile phone, a set of brand-new kitchen knives still in their original packaging. Others just ask for a few cents for something to eat or a place to sleep; apparently that's how it is when you live on the ground floor and like to keep the window open. My boyfriend doesn't like being on display, he says, but for some reason I like it when the people outside turn their heads and say to each other it looks nice in here. The wall behind me is covered with books on shelves, and the extra pleasure I get from showing them off, again, probably has to do with my father, since pretty much every book in our house when I was a child belonged to him. Maybe I just need to hear it from the people out there since sometimes I can hardly believe it myself, that no matter how fucked up I feel, I still managed to build this home with someone I love, someone who knows me better than anyone else, and who I actually dare believe loves me back. For a while we even considered having our own children together, but he ended up saying no, and in the end, it was probably for the better. I'll never know what kind of father I'd have become myself, but if this hurt can really be passed down, I'm glad that the cycle ends here. I get that lots of people think I should reach out now before it's too late, seeing as my father is 67 years old and already has a heart attack and skin cancer behind him, that I'll regret it later if we never talk it out, but I'm too afraid he's like an onion of lies, that when you peel back a layer, there'll just be more lies under it. The primary condition for love must be the ability to stand by one's most vulnerable self, and all I can do now is insist on living by this honesty myself. I have a list of things I need to confess to my boyfriend before this book goes to print, and I started last week by telling him about the guy who raped me for hours while I was unconscious, and even though my boyfriend was hurt that I hadn't felt safe enough to share this with him before, I reassured him it was never so much about my fear of his reaction as it was about my own need for denial. Fortunately, we have the advantage that honesty is actually an option between my boyfriend and I. He made it clear on our first date that he never wanted a monogamous relationship, and even though I was used to people assuming it rather than talking about it, it was how I felt too. I still remember how liberating it was when I first found a word for my desires that no longer sounded like an excuse. It was back when Andreas and I still had our band together, and we scored an opening gig for Kids on TV in Christiania, and the next day, we hung out with the band and had lunch at a Mediterranean place where the buffet was drowning in oil, and one of the members told us about how he started the band after years of his life following one partner in and out of hospitals with one AIDS-related disease after another, until 1996 when he finally got the pills that worked, and they both got their lives back, and they both got their hunger for love back, both together and each on their own, and he paused, looked at me, and said he just assumed I was polyamorous too, and I nodded because even though I'd never heard the word before, I understood right away that I'd been lacking it. I knew it had always been a lie when I defended my desires by saying sex was just sex and that was all it was, while at the same time I infused every kiss and every fuck with layer upon layer of meaning, and almost every time it was this meaning I craved more than the body underneath. I want us to grow old together but I don't want a fence around our love, and the butterflies my boyfriend has in his stomach over somebody else just fill me with confidence because of the trust it shows when he shares it, and I hope to learn this from him, to share everything with the kind of trust and vulnerability I have always loved and admired him for. This book may be read as a commitment, but I'm running out of pages here, and we still have a happy ending to get through. Some will surely find it tacked on, like Rushdie who doesn't buy that Dorothy actually longs to get back to Kansas, and I'll be the first to admit that my attempt at bringing it home with plot structure is nowhere near as convincing as *Pulp Fiction*, but there's no one I need to convince here, and since the story is mine, I also get to decide where it ends. I've chosen to end it in Berlin. On a summer night in 2013. I've just said goodbye to Antoine, a small petite guy with jet-black hair and big Bambi eyes who I had a thing going with that summer. I had quite a few things going that summer, but Antoine was the last one, and as I get home after our goodbye I feel a tinge of emptiness in my chest, but also a belief that even though every ending isn't always a new beginning, the emptiness I sit with on this night still holds potential. Five weeks later, I am sitting with my boyfriend on a balcony in Schöneberg sipping rum and cola while a fetish festival is happening in the streets outside. My friend, who's an artist, is having an open house, and even though there's 25,000 fetish guys going about in the streets outside, all I want to do is sit here on the balcony and drink rum and cola with the most fantastic person I've only just met. Three years later I cycle past that same house and look up at the balconies, trying to tell one from another, because my friend who's an artist is also the neighbour of the guy who raped me for hours while I was unconscious, and actually, this is probably why I go past here, to see if I can tell the balconies apart, the one where I sat with my boyfriend drinking rum and cola, and the one I just lay behind and got raped for hours while I was unconscious, and held up against such moments, the emptiness I feel as I give up feels rather like indifference, as if my body resigns itself to being nothing but an object that can be swept back and forth, as if it makes no difference where it ends up (like the roulette wheel spinning; red, black, red, black, loves me, loves me not). But fortunately, this is not where it ends. I'm back in 2013, in the night that does end up as a new beginning. I've gone to a party to dance on my own, taken one line of speed, not to get high but to avoid getting wasted from the drink tokens they still hand me at the door because I used to play music here, back when heartbroken boys with guitars were still a thing we danced to. It's five in the morning now, and the party has gathered in the lounge. We continue dancing to romantic film anthems from the eighties, and this is when he first smiles at me, shy and intoxicated, like a fallen superhero looking for someone to lean on. Later he tells me that his friends had gone home, and he'd stayed there only for me, and this is why he got so drunk, since he isn't used to being out by himself. He seems so pure and innocent that I almost feel guilty for things I haven't even done yet, but then he leans towards me, like a rose asking to be picked, and I decide to take the chance. The morning after, it's me who asks to see him again, and today, eight years later, he's still my best bet for a happy ending because happy endings aren't really endings, not permanent states, but merely the beginning of everything we still have to fight for together, and even though our desires may never be like they were back then (like the morning after our first New Year's together when we sat in the back of the bus together, electrified with anticipation of soon being naked together, of all the marks he was going to leave on my butt with the riding crop we got from the sports shop together), I'd argue that we have something much deeper together, and sure, my ending may not be as romantic as Romeo and Juliet's, but I'd also argue that, in the end, Romeo doesn't have a clue what love is about. It's romantic to run away with someone you just met at a party, but it has nothing to do with love. It's romantic to drink poison and die holding each other, but it has even less to do with love. It's romantic to lose yourself in a random boy, in a random night, in a park, in his skin, in drugs, and in red spots, but it hasn't the faintest thing to do with love. It's romantic to bleed to death in a bathroom at the Chelsea Hotel, it's romantic to put a shotgun in your mouth and pull the trigger while Neil Young sings in the background that it's better to burn out than to fade away, and yet, it's as far from love as anything can possibly get. Where romance loves its wrecks and ruins, love at least must have the will to erect, and though love itself never conquers anything, it makes us stronger every time we choose it, since love is not a prize given to those who fight long enough for the cause, but a choice we make over and over, and this is what I'm trying to say here, that I'm dedicated to our love (dedicated to you) because I still believe that we're greater together, that we can build each other up to be more than we are on our own, even though the world is a fucked up place, and in the end, I don't believe anything means anything.

# FILM

Romeo + Juliet
1996, Baz Luhrmann

My Own Private Idaho
1991, Gus Van Sant

Raspberry Reich
2004, Bruce LaBruce

The Living End
1992, Gregg Araki

The Wizard of Oz
1939, Victor Fleming

Tropfen auf heiße Steine
2000, François Ozon

La Chinoise
1967, Jean Luc Godard

Pulp Fiction
1994, Quentin Tarantino

Crybaby
1990, John Waters

Hannibal & Jerry
1997, Michael Wikke og Steen Rasmussen

Trois Couleurs: Bleu, Blanc, Rouge
1993-94, Krzysztof Kieslowski

Thelma & Louise
1991, Ridley Scott

Bonnie and Clyde
1967, Arthur Penn

Party Monster
2003, Fenton Bailey og Randy Barbato

# SOUNDTRACK

Blueboy – So Catch Him
Belle & Sebastian – Too Much Love
Bright Eyes – A Perfect Sonnet
Sonic Youth – Kotton Crown
Leonard Cohen – First We Take Manhattan
My Favourite – 17 Berlin
Bronski Beat – Smalltown Boy
Pet Shop Boys – New York City Boy
The Cure – Strange Attraction
Lana Del Rey – California
Joanna Newsom – Good Intentions Paving Company
Lisa Germano – Bruises
Portishead – Sour Times
My Bloody Valentine – Sueisfine
Sonic Youth – Teenage Riot
Belle & Sebastian – Me and the Major
Saint Etienne – Sylvie
Tiga & Zyntherious – Sunglasses at Night
Erasure – A Little Respect
Pet Shop Boys – Go West
Boy Harsher – LA
Air – All I need
Søn – Maveskind
Lana Del Rey – White Dress
Neil Young – Hey Hey, My My
Abba – Mamma Mia
Judy Garland – Somewhere Over the Rainbow